P9-DIG-091

DISCARD

pocket.watch

RYAN'S WORLD

RED TITAN
AND THE FLOOR OF LAVA

SIMON SPOTLIGHT
An imprint of Simon & Schuster Children's Publishing Division
1230 Avenue of the Americas, New York, New York 10020
This Simon Spotlight edition May 2022
Text by Arie Kaplan

TM & © 2022 RTR Production, LLC, RFR Entertainment, Inc. and Remka, Inc., and
PocketWatch, Inc. Ryan ToysReview, Ryan's World and all related titles, logos and
characters are trademarks of RTR Production, LLC, RFR Entertainment, Inc. and Remka,
Inc. The pocket.watch logo and all related titles, logos and characters are trademarks of
PocketWatch, Inc. All Rights Reserved. Photos and illustrations of Ryan and Ryan's World
characters copyright © RTR Production, LLC, RFR Entertainment, Inc. and Remka, Inc.
All rights reserved, including the right of reproduction in whole or in part in any form.
SIMON SPOTLIGHT, READY-TO-READ, and colophon are registered trademarks of
Simon & Schuster, Inc.
For more information about special discounts for bulk purchases, please contact
Simon & Schuster Special Sales at 1-866-506-1949 or business@simonandschuster.com.
Manufactured in China 0222 SCP
2 4 6 8 10 9 7 5 3 1
ISBN 978-1-6659-1359-1 (hc)
ISBN 978-1-6659-1358-4 (pbk)
ISBN 978-1-6659-1360-7 (ebook)

RED TITAN
AND THE FLOOR OF LAVA

by **RYAN KAJI**
written by **ARIE KAPLAN**
illustrated by **PATRICK SPAZIANTE**

Ready-to-Read *GRAPHICS*

Simon Spotlight
New York   London   Toronto   Sydney   New Delhi

HOW TO READ THIS BOOK

Ryan is here to give you some tips on reading this book.

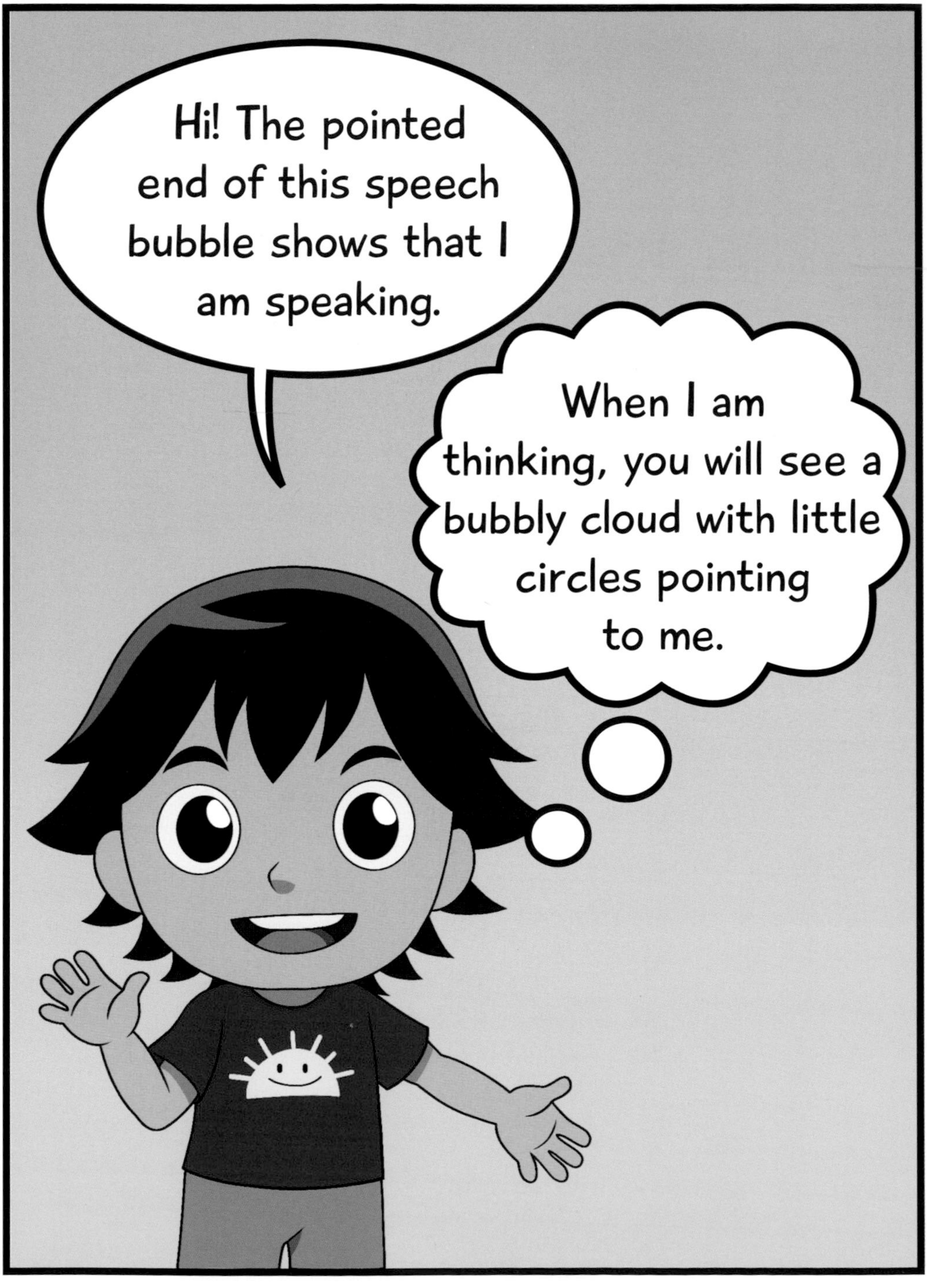
Hi! The pointed end of this speech bubble shows that I am speaking.
When I am thinking, you will see a bubbly cloud with little circles pointing to me.

R0464054251

It was a beautiful day. Ryan, Peck, and Combo Panda were on their way to a picnic.

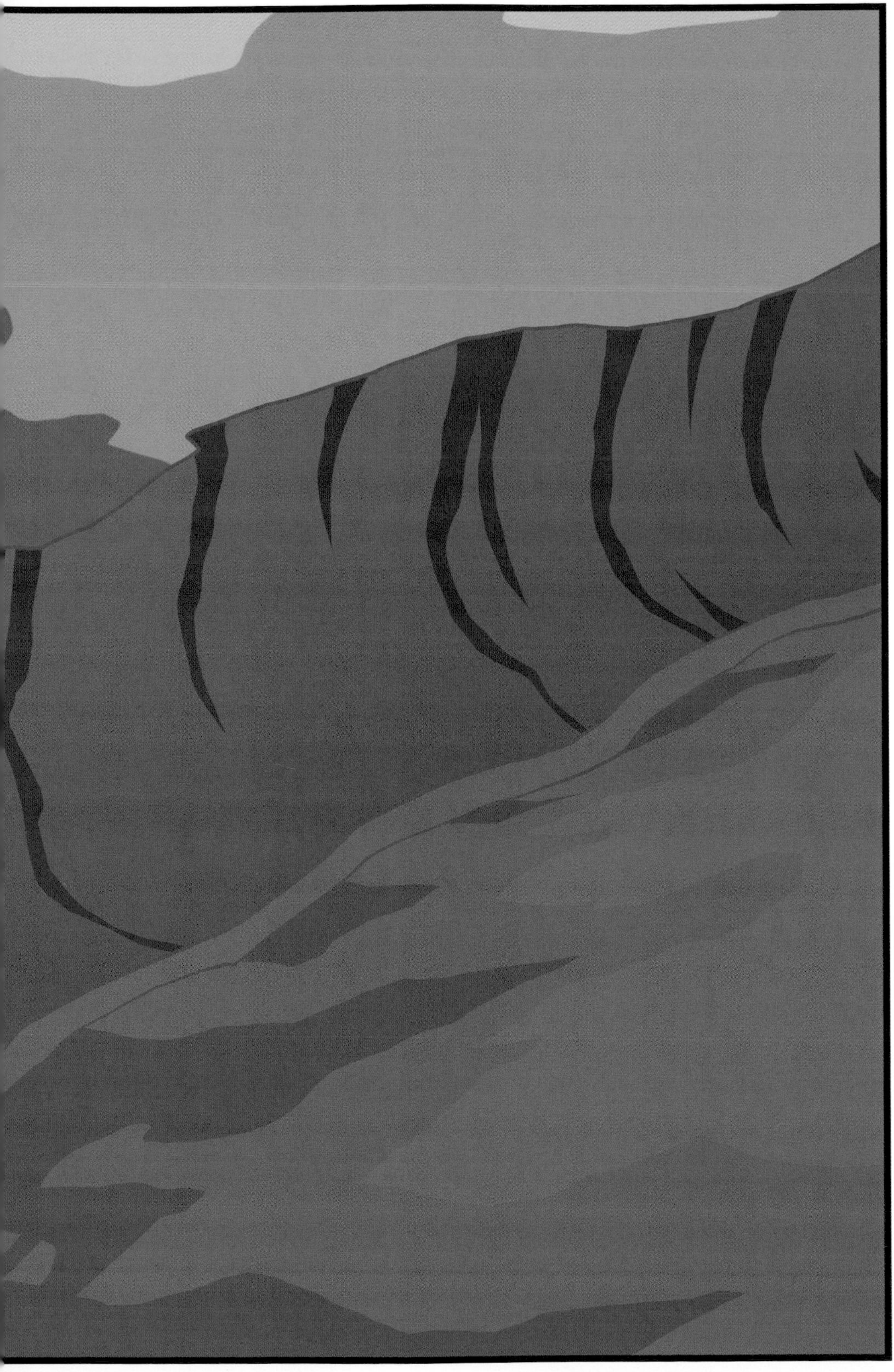

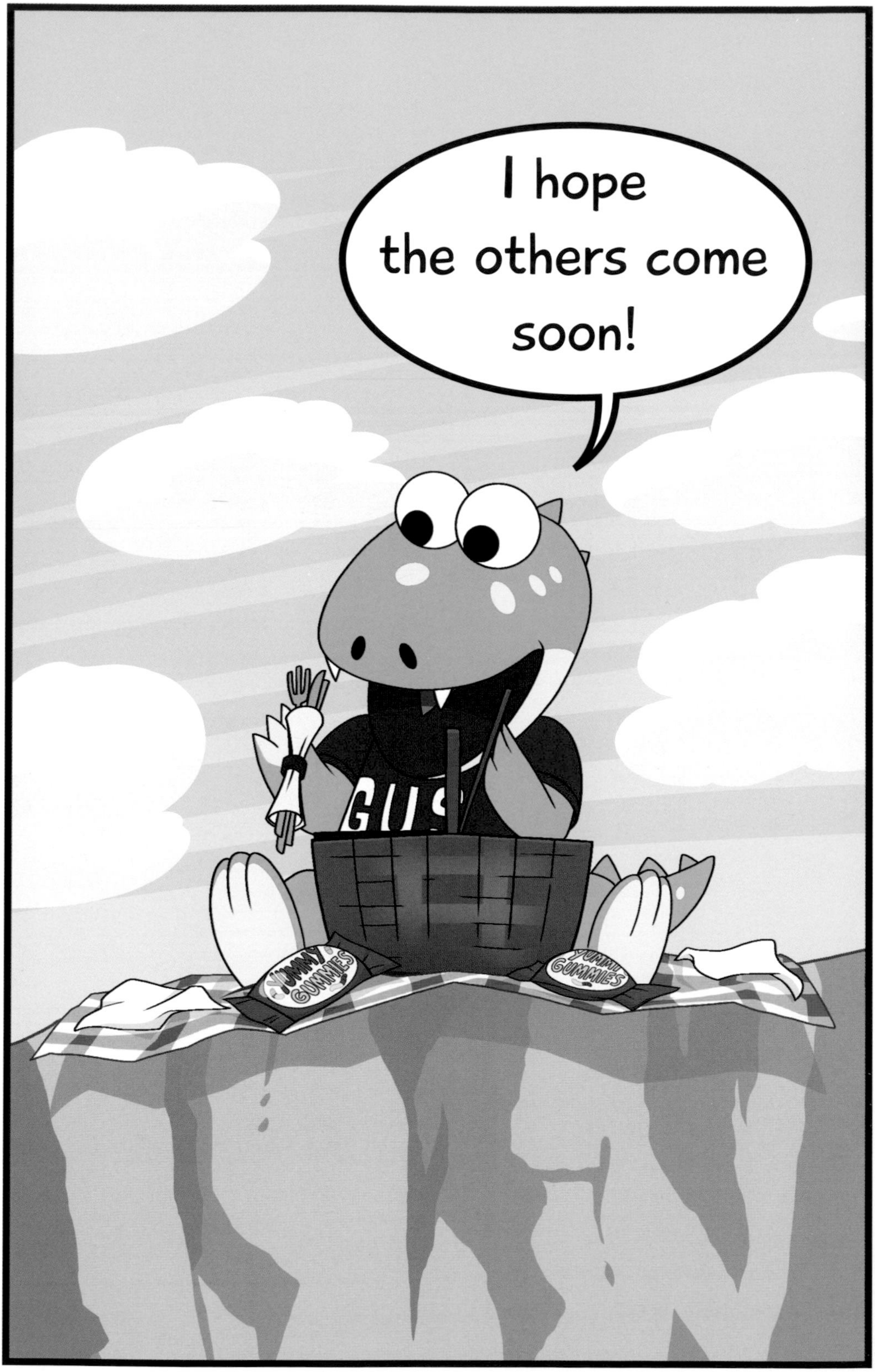
I hope the others come soon!
GUS
YUMMY GUMMIES
YUMMY GUMMIES

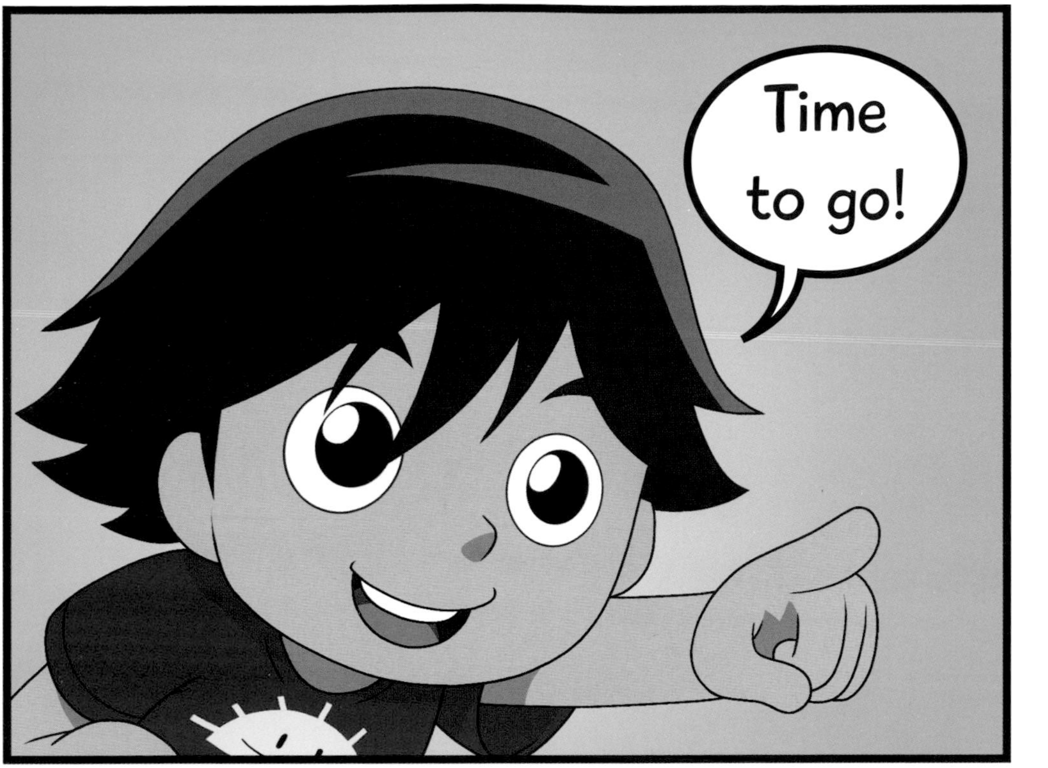
Time to go!

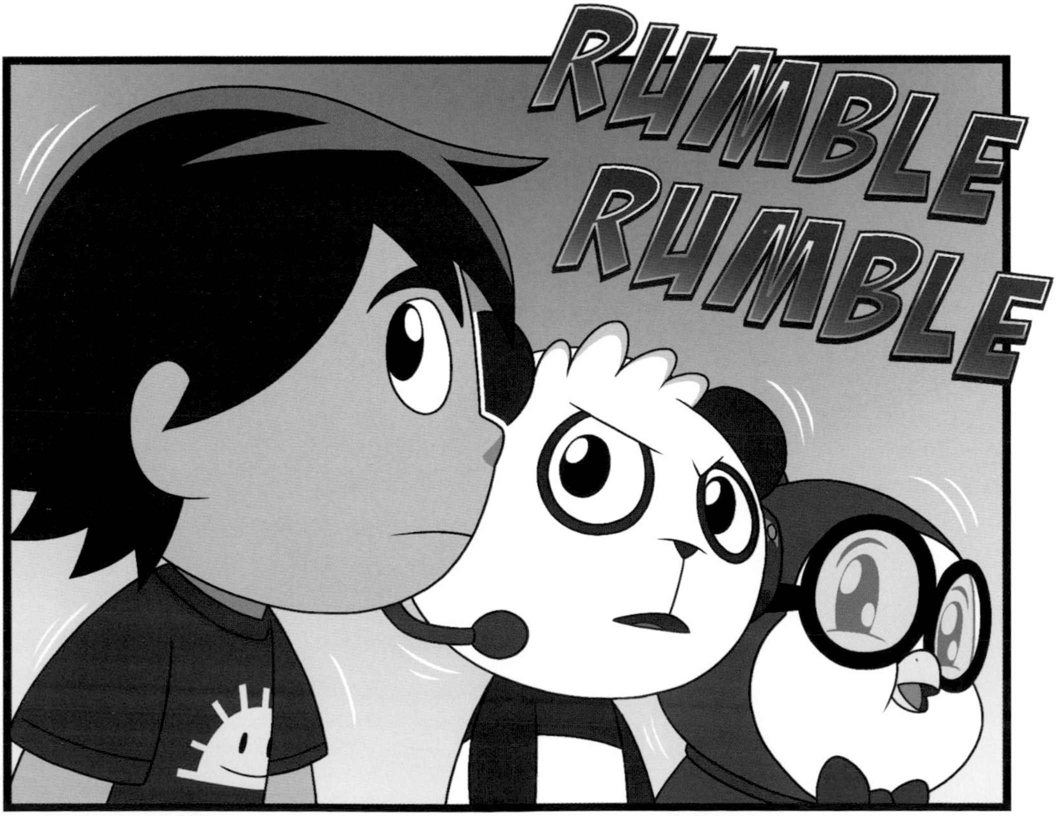
RUMBLE RUMBLE

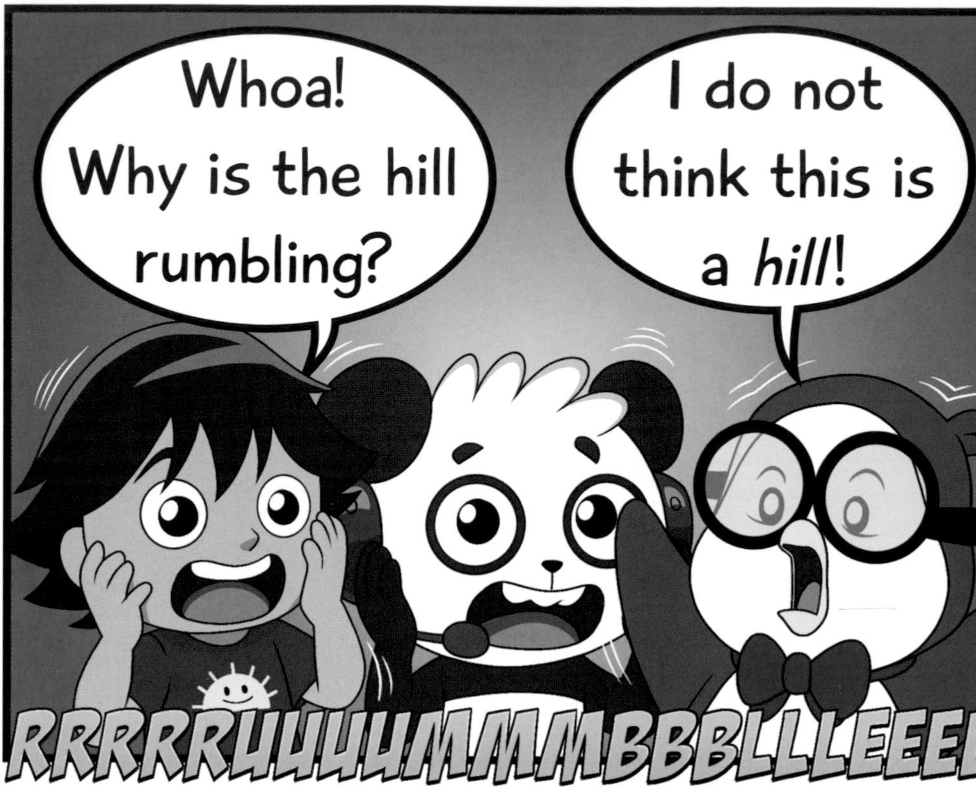
Whoa! Why is the hill rumbling?
I do not think this is a *hill*!
RRRRRUUUUUMMMMBBBLLLEEEE

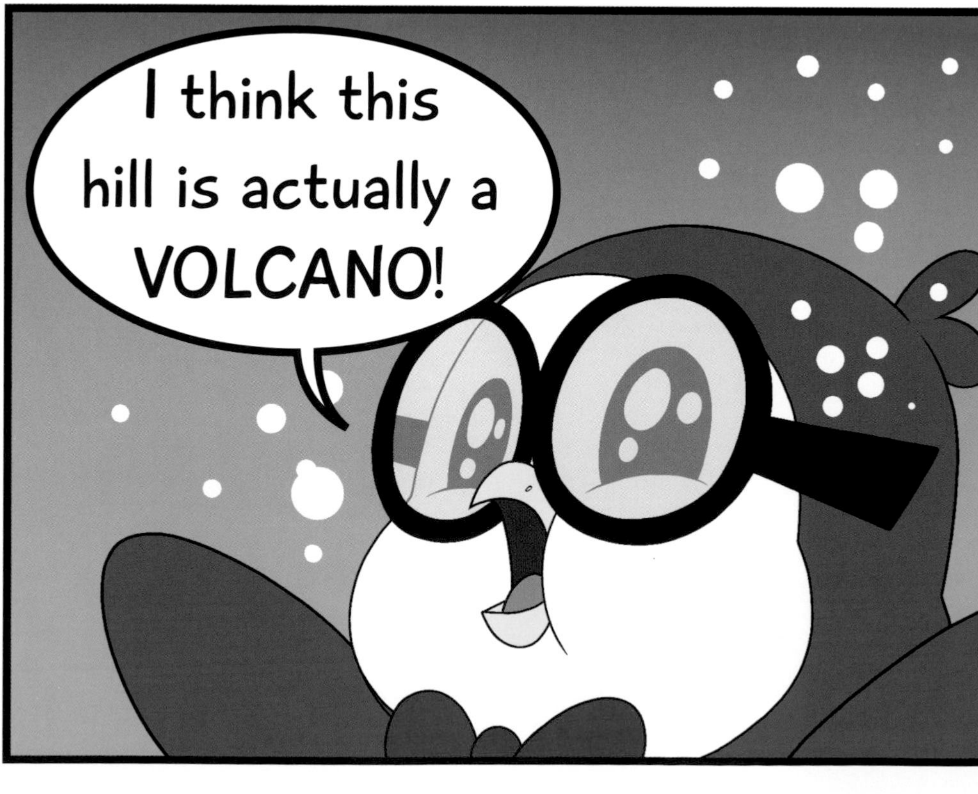
I think this hill is actually a VOLCANO!

Meanwhile, at the top of the hill...

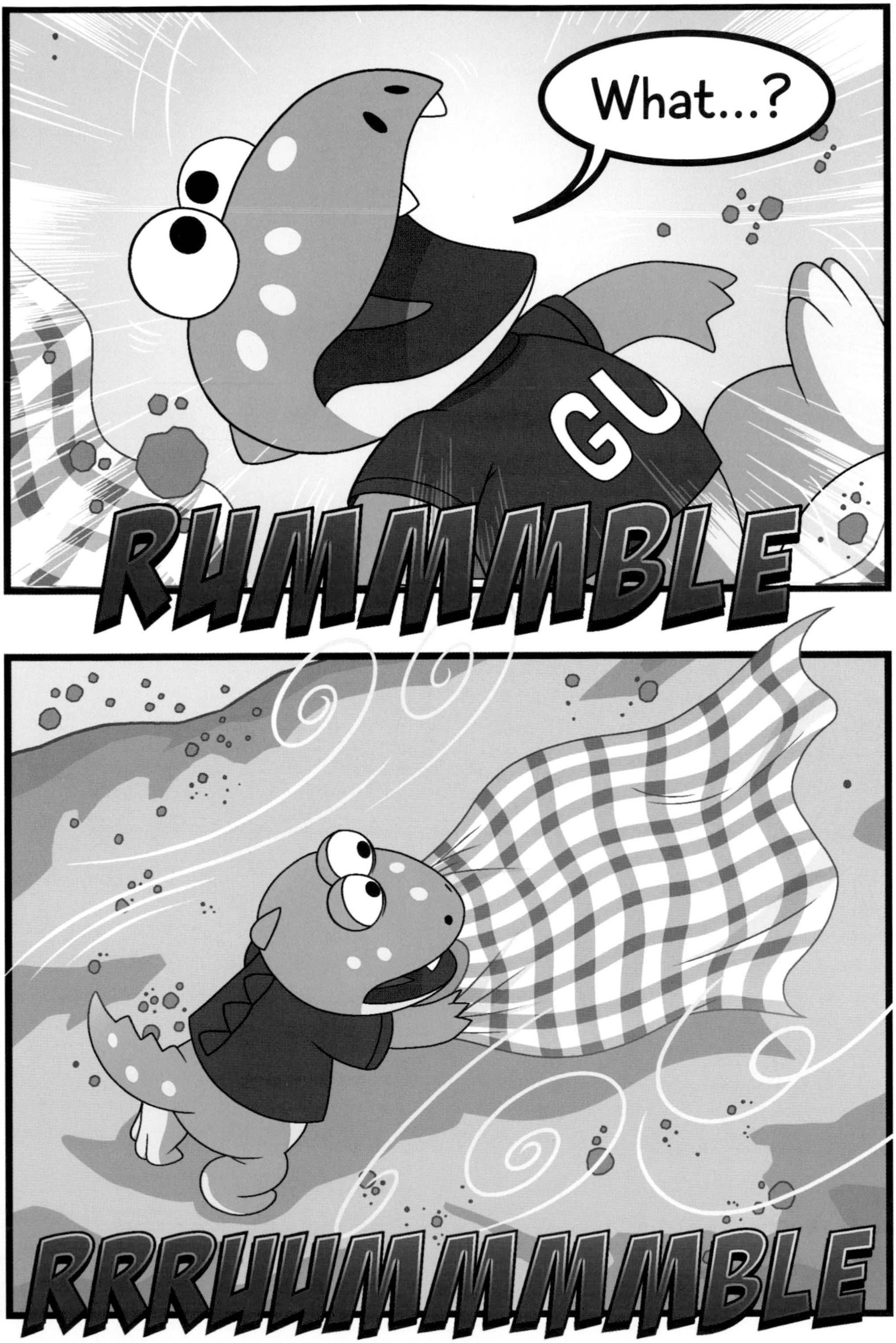
What...?
GU
RUMMMBLE
RRRUUMMMMMBLE

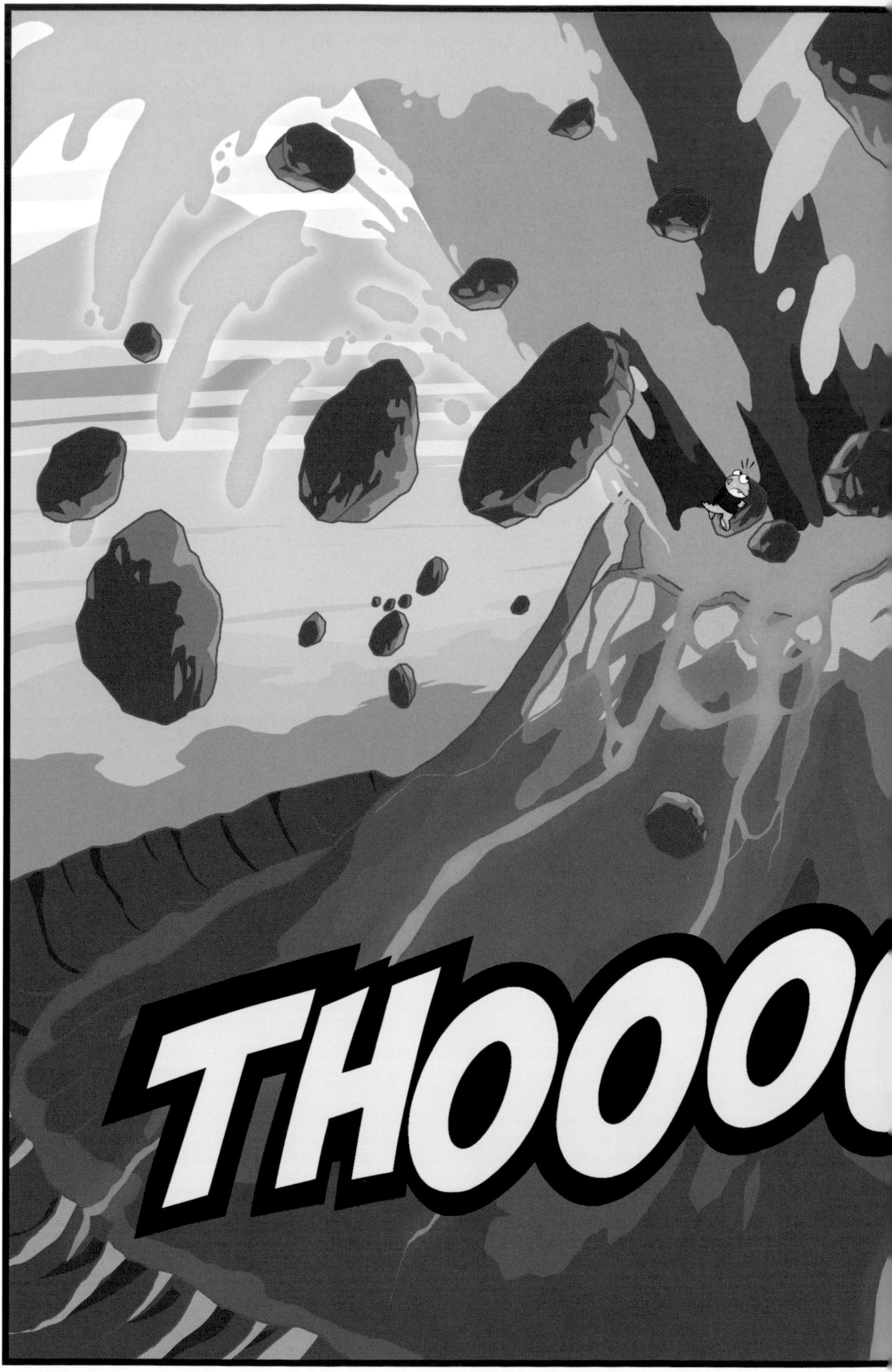
THOOO

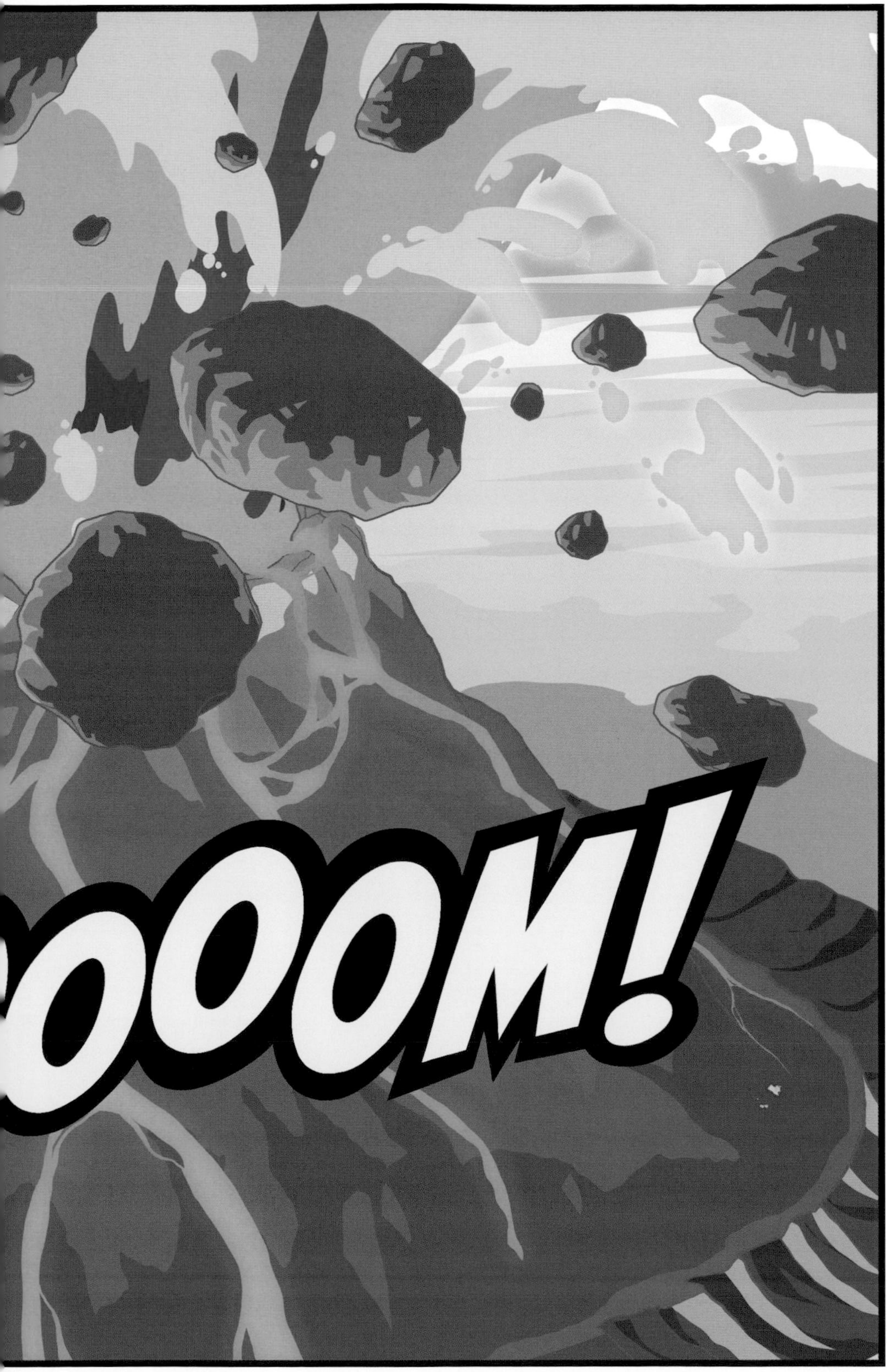
OOOM!

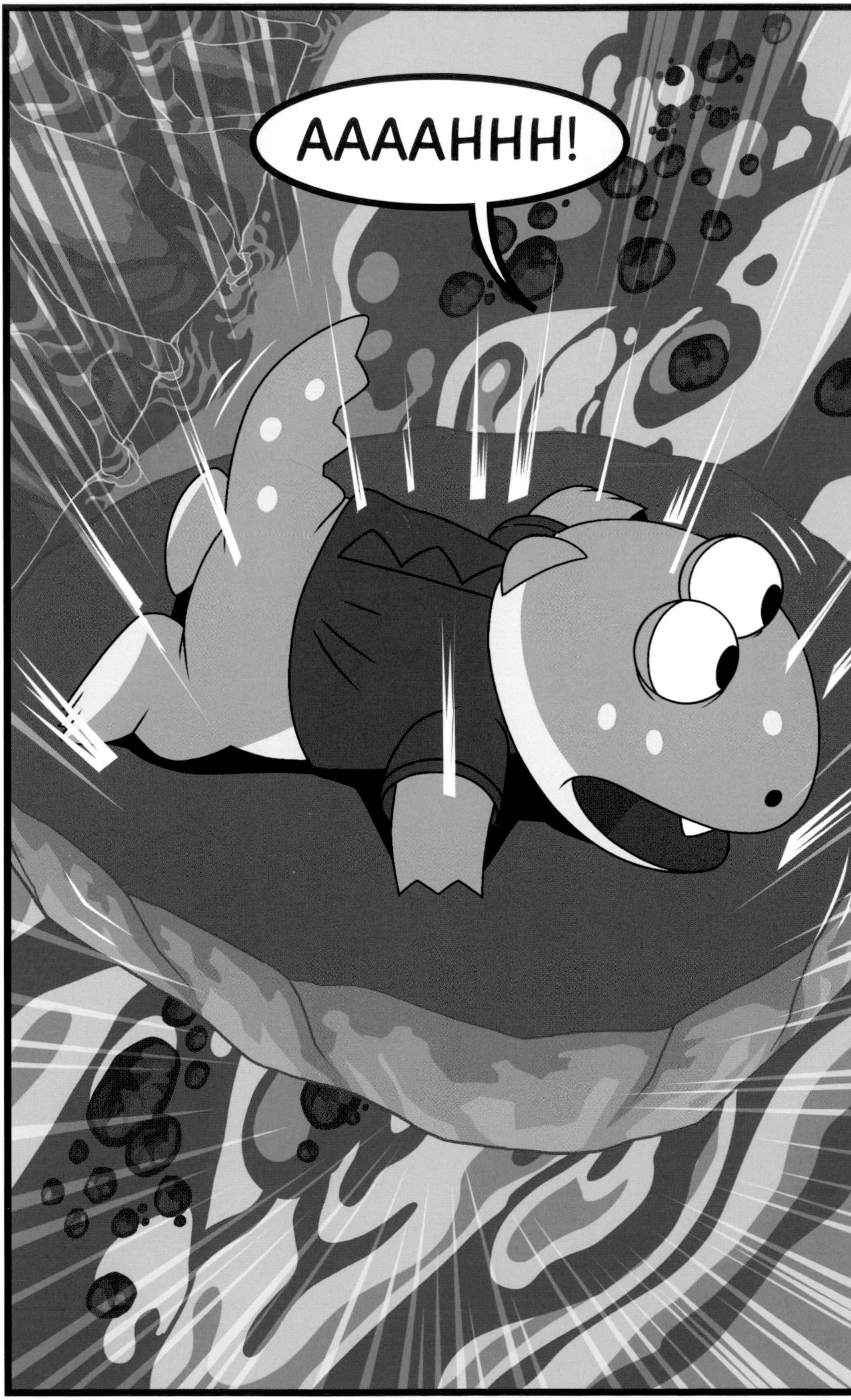
AAAAHHH!

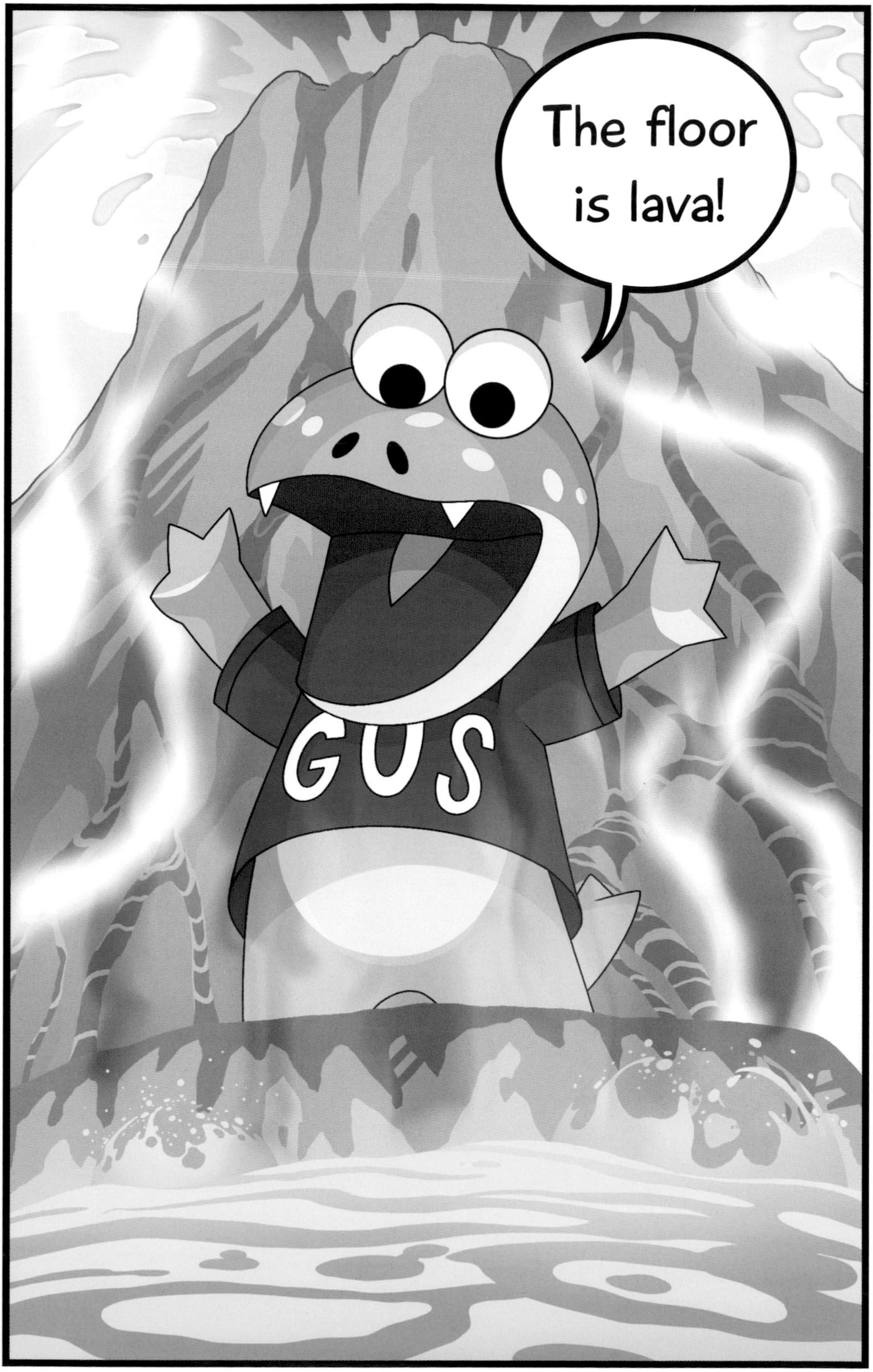
The floor is lava!
GUS

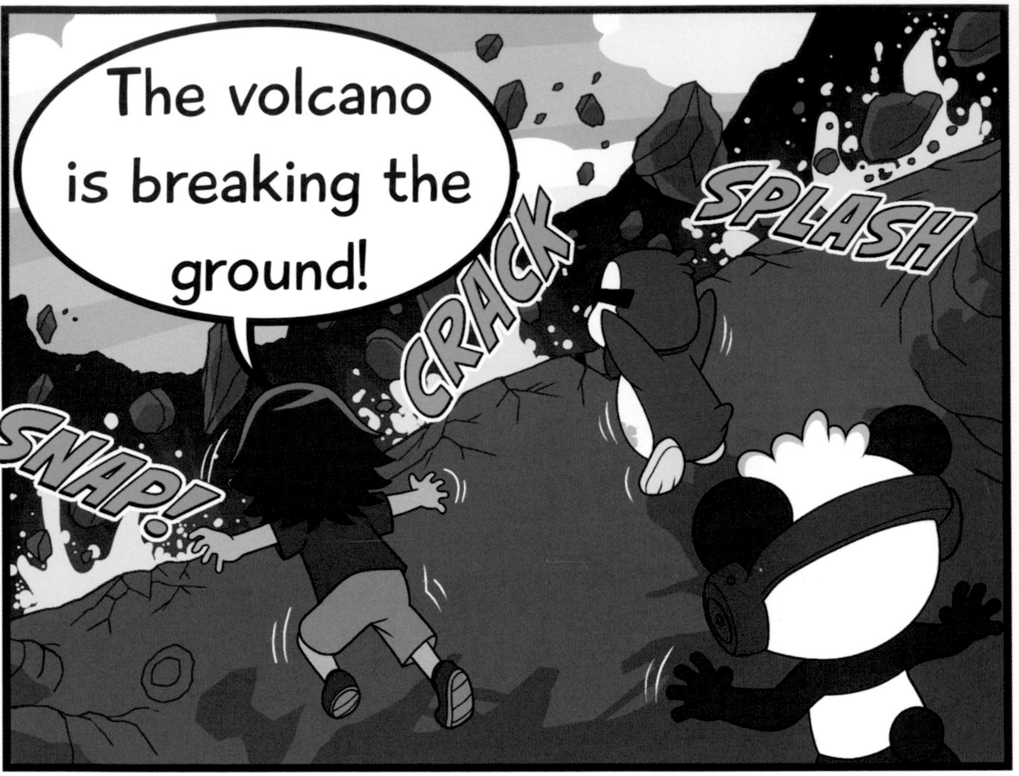
The volcano is breaking the ground!
CRACK
SPLASH
SNAP!

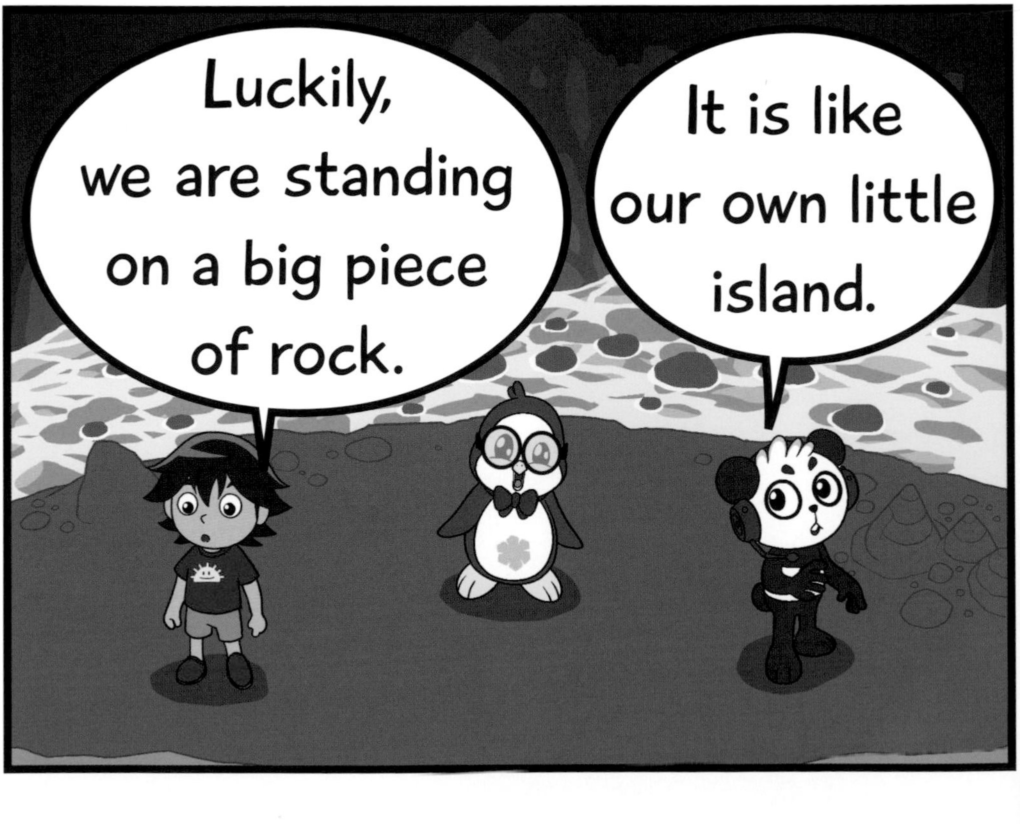
Luckily, we are standing on a big piece of rock.
It is like our own little island.

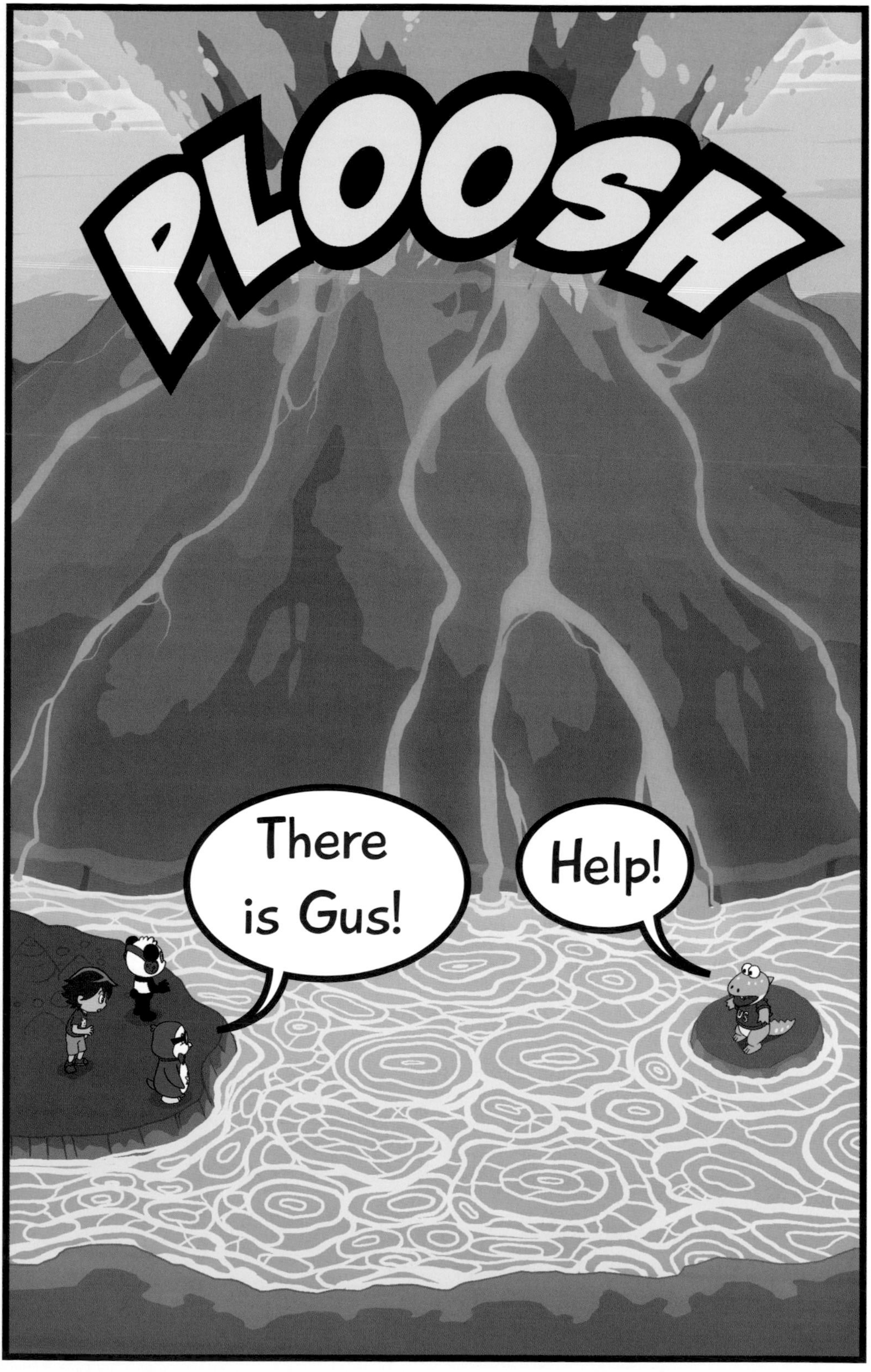
PLOOSH
There is Gus!
Help!

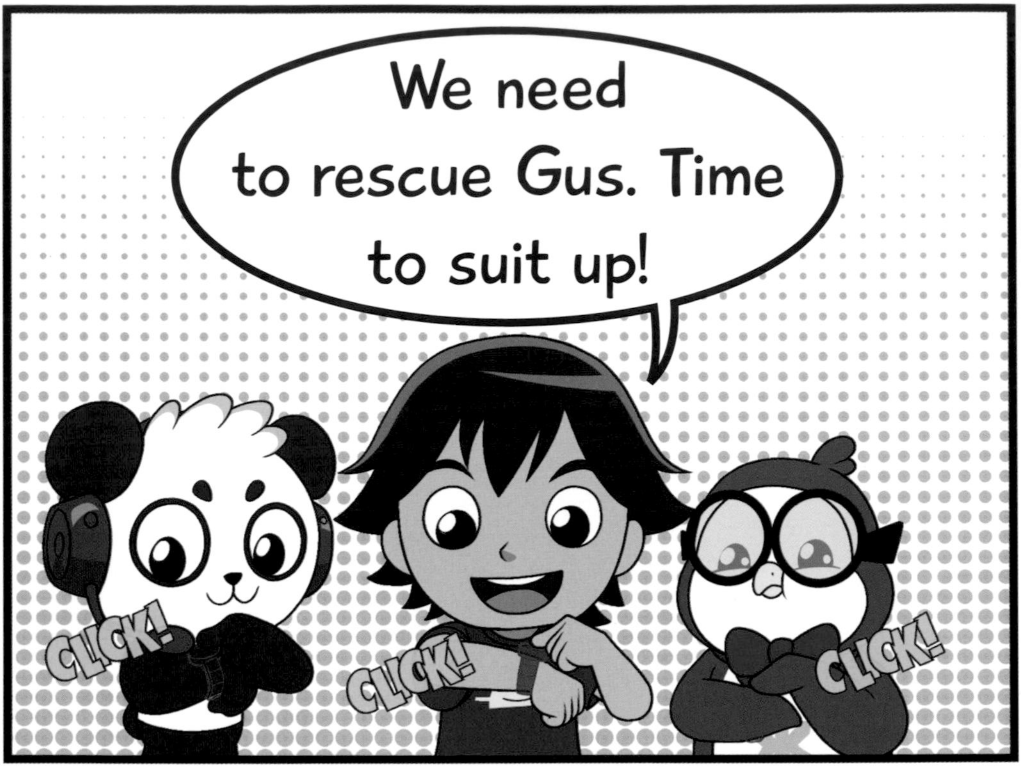
We need to rescue Gus. Time to suit up!
CLICK!
CLICK!
CLICK!

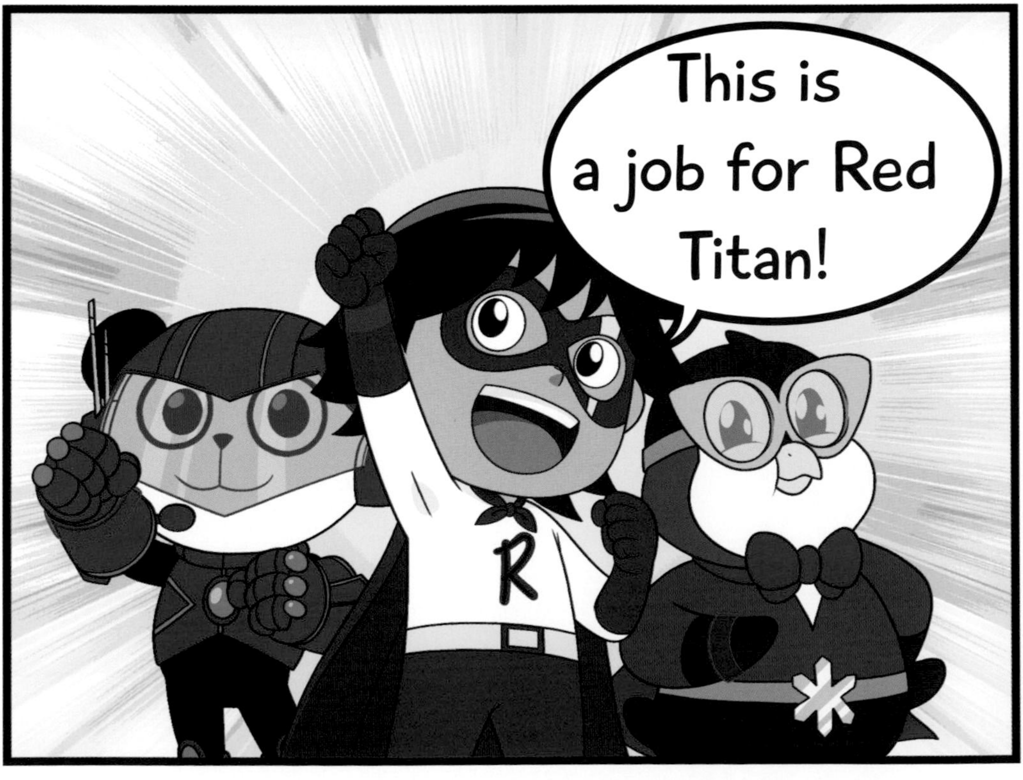
This is a job for Red Titan!
R

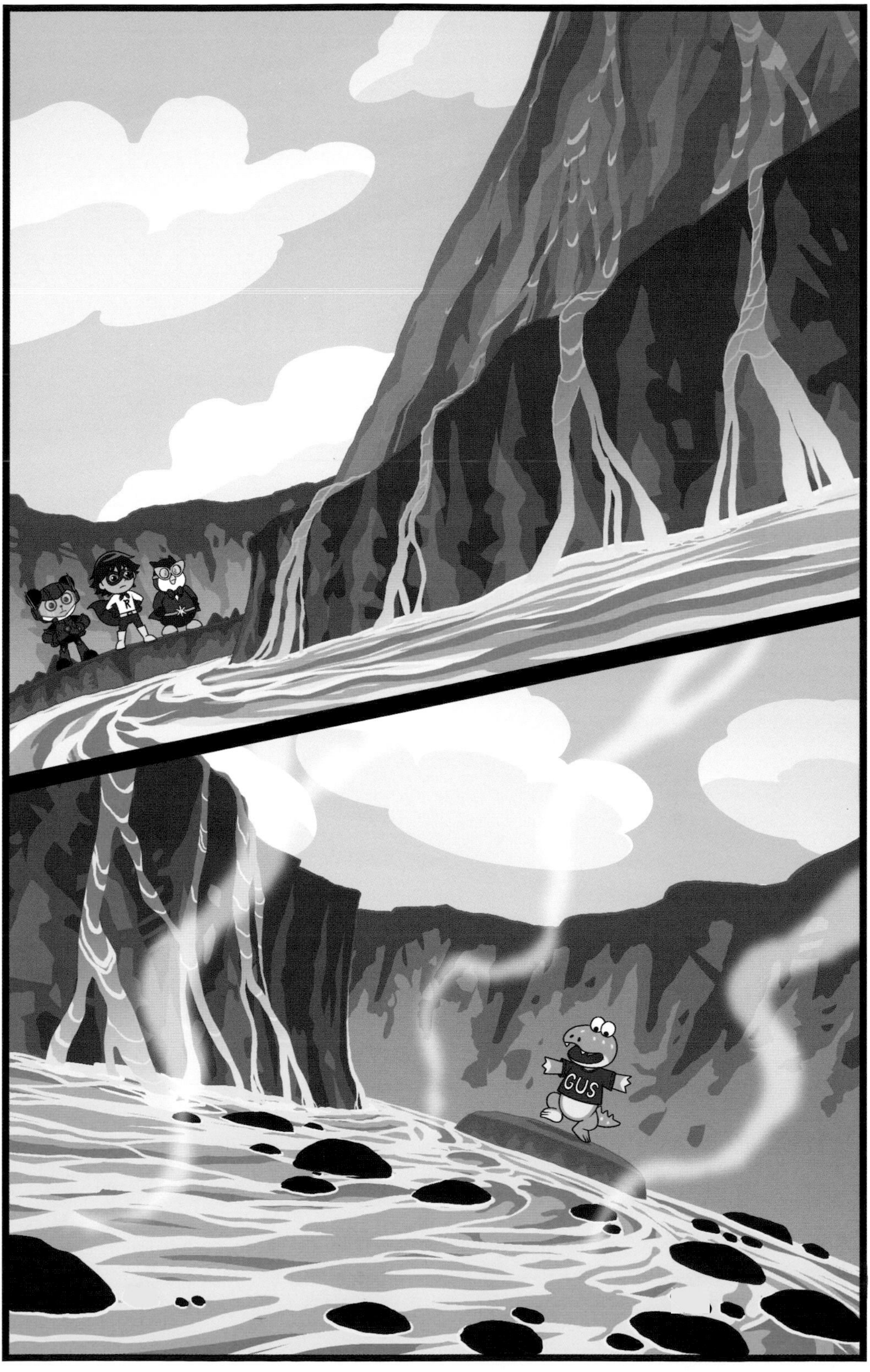
GUS

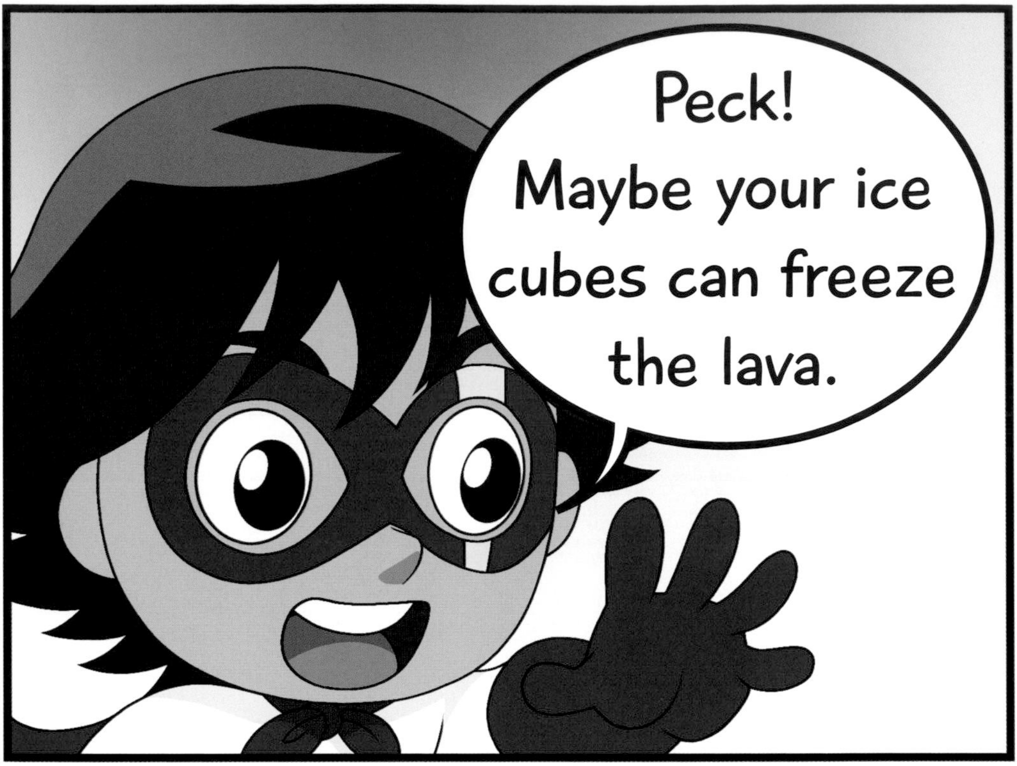
Peck!
Maybe your ice cubes can freeze the lava.

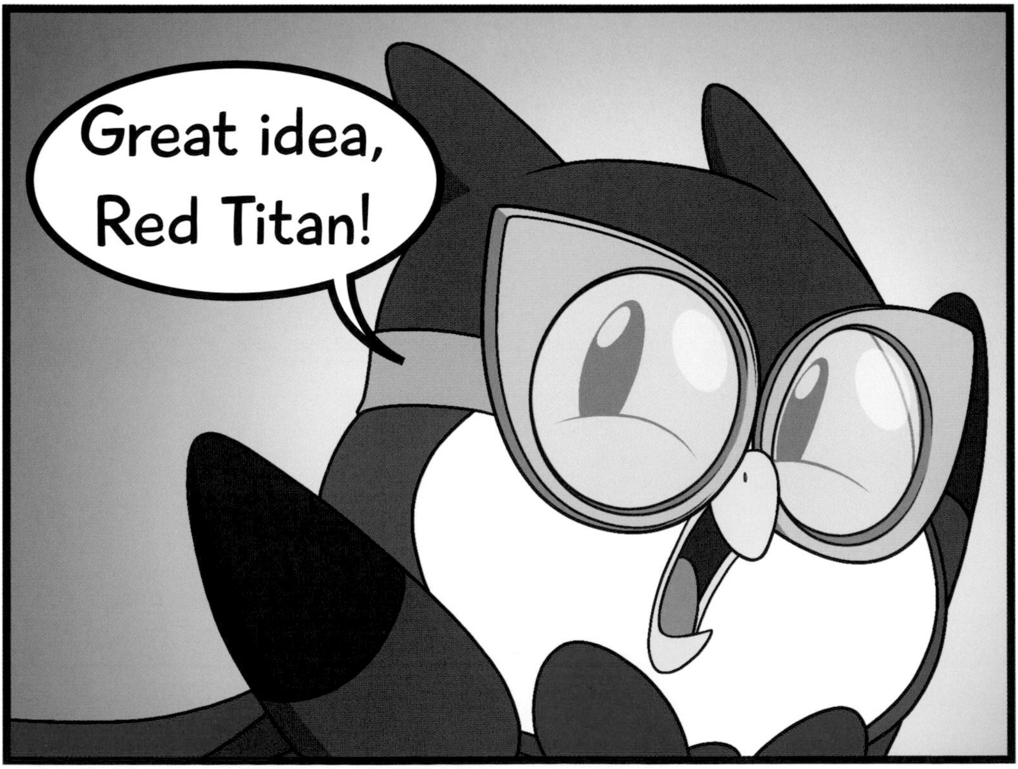
Great idea, Red Titan!

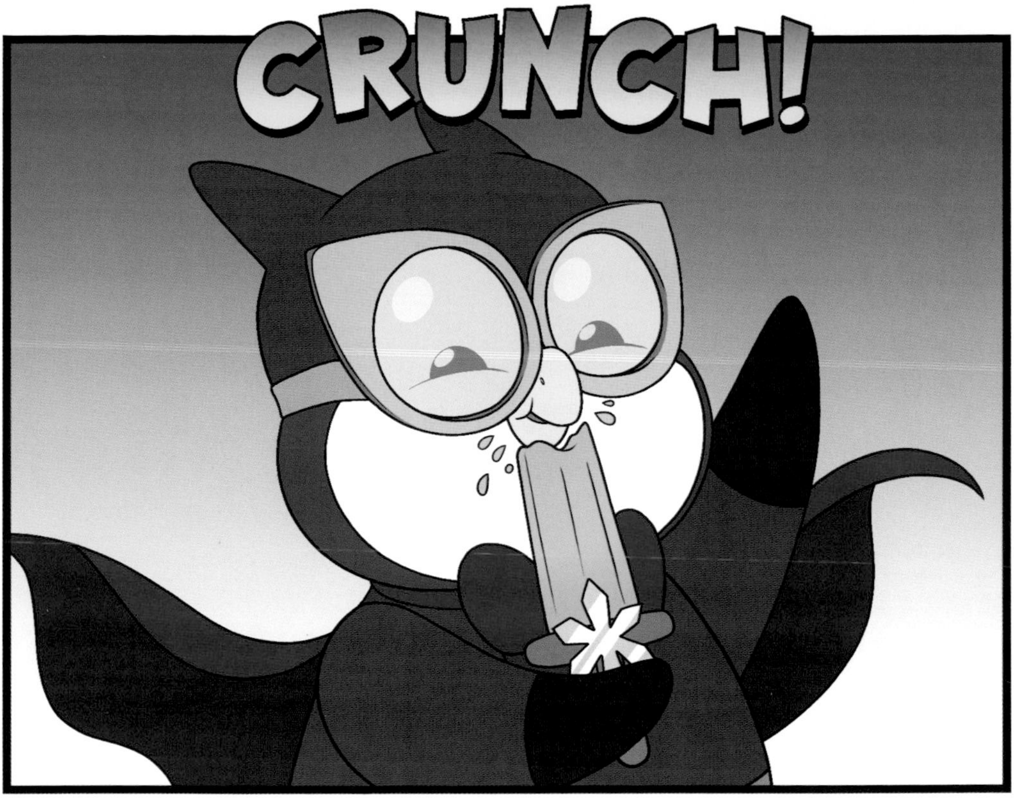
CRUNCH!

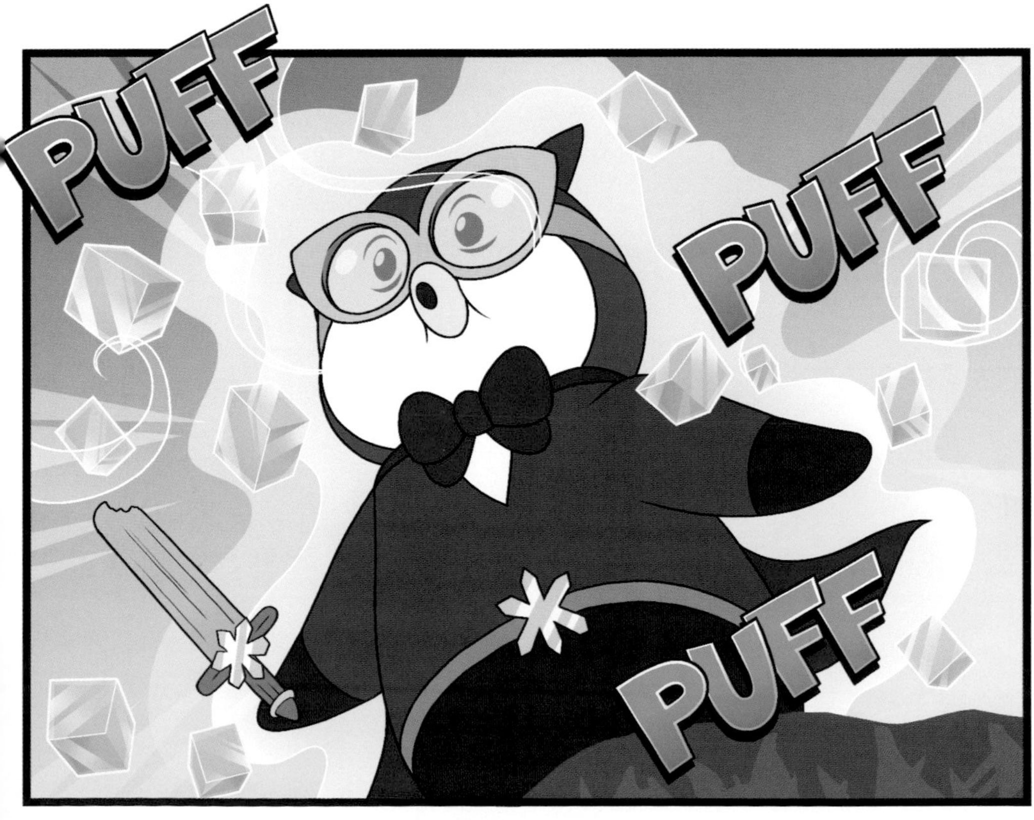
PUFF
PUFF
PUFF

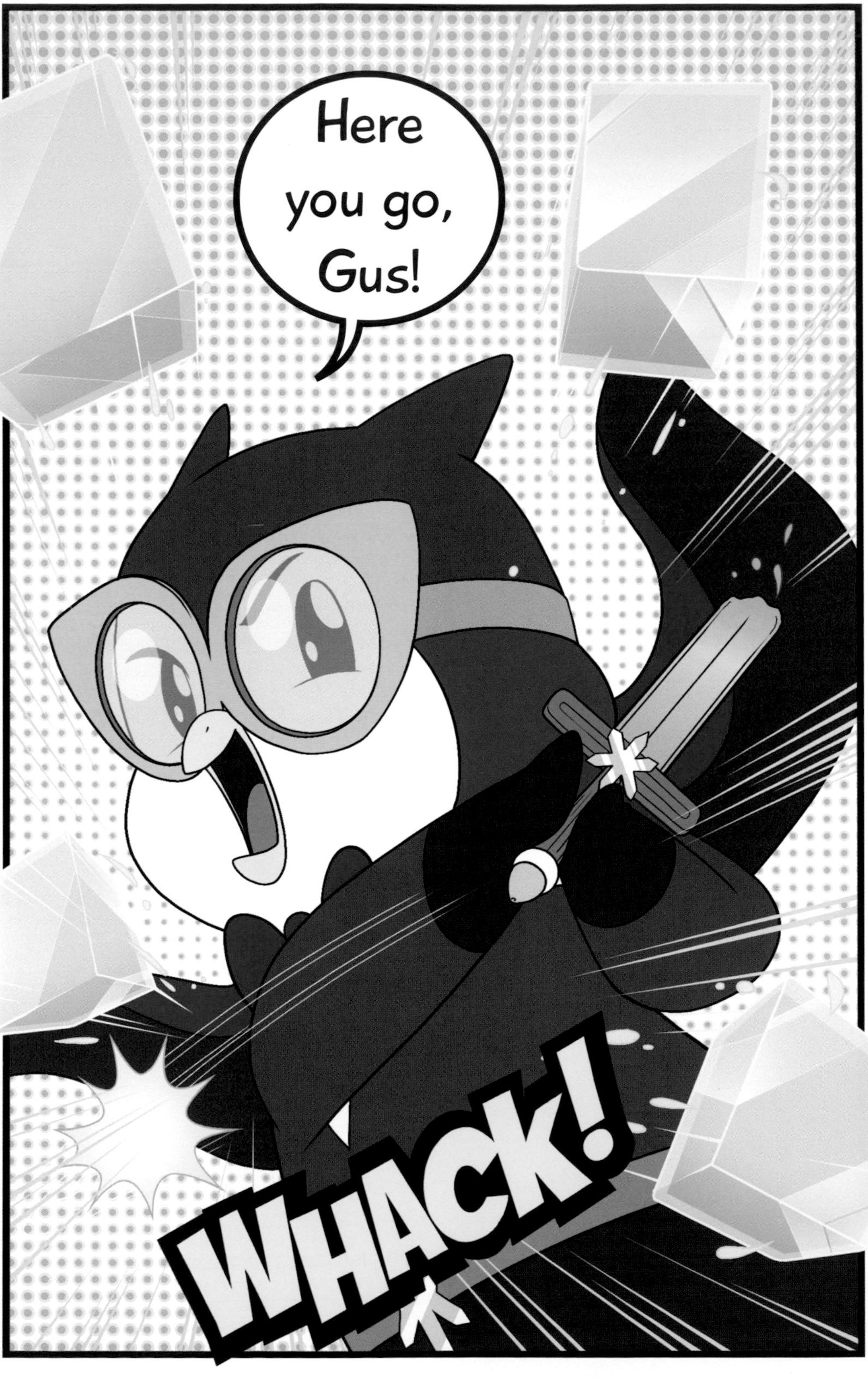
Here you go, Gus!
WHACK!

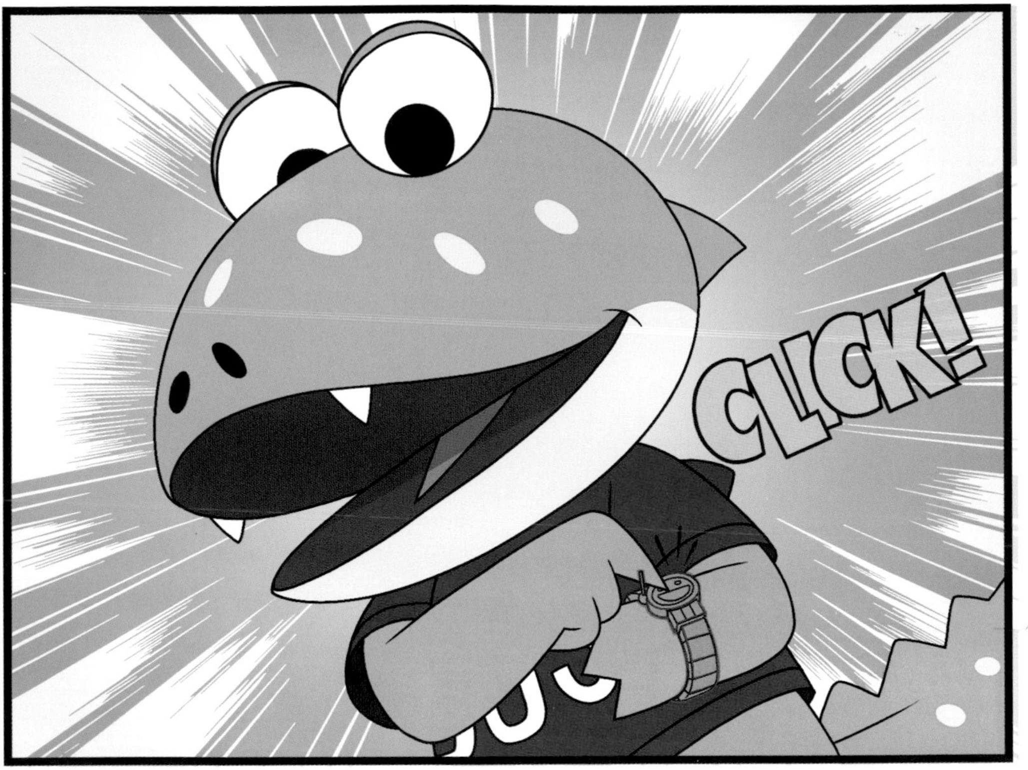
CLICK!

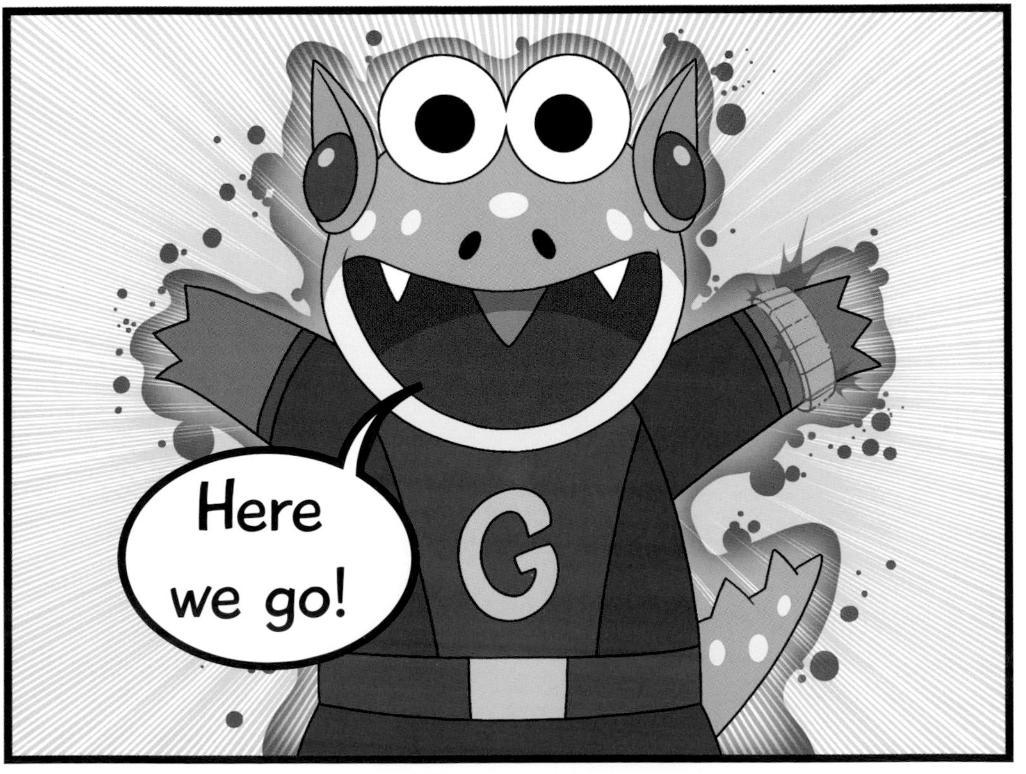
Here we go!

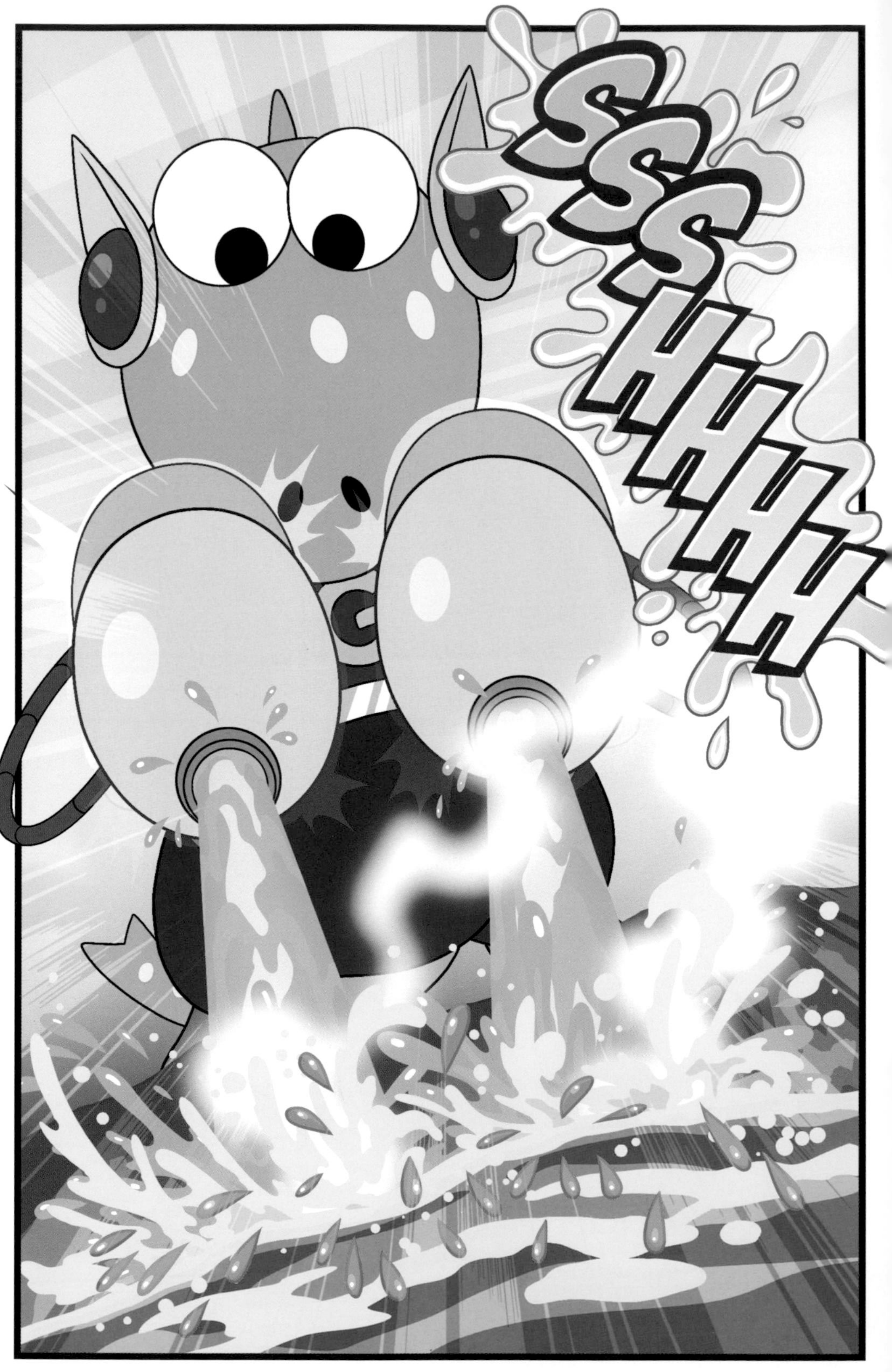
SSSHHHHH

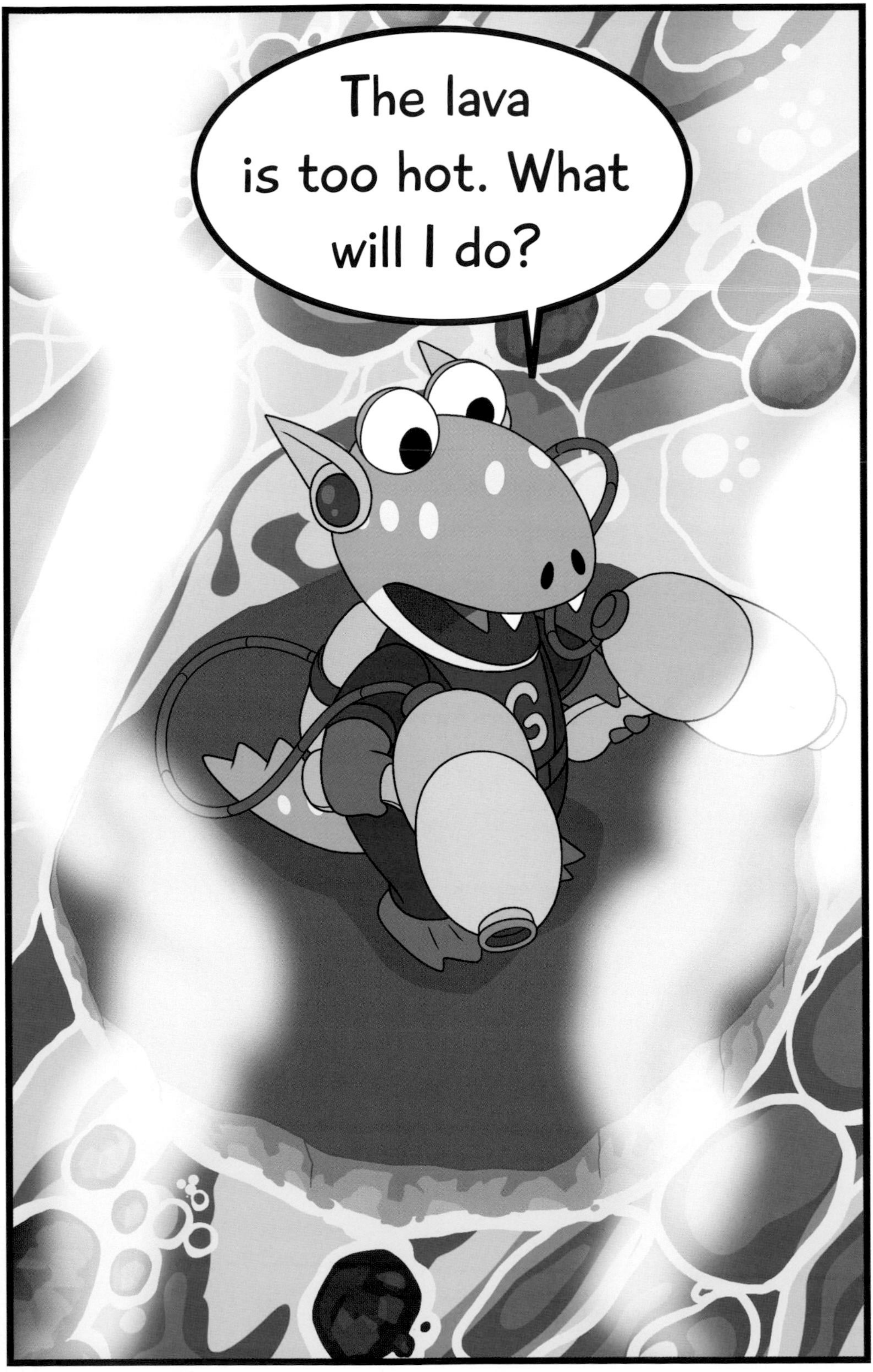
The lava is too hot. What will I do?

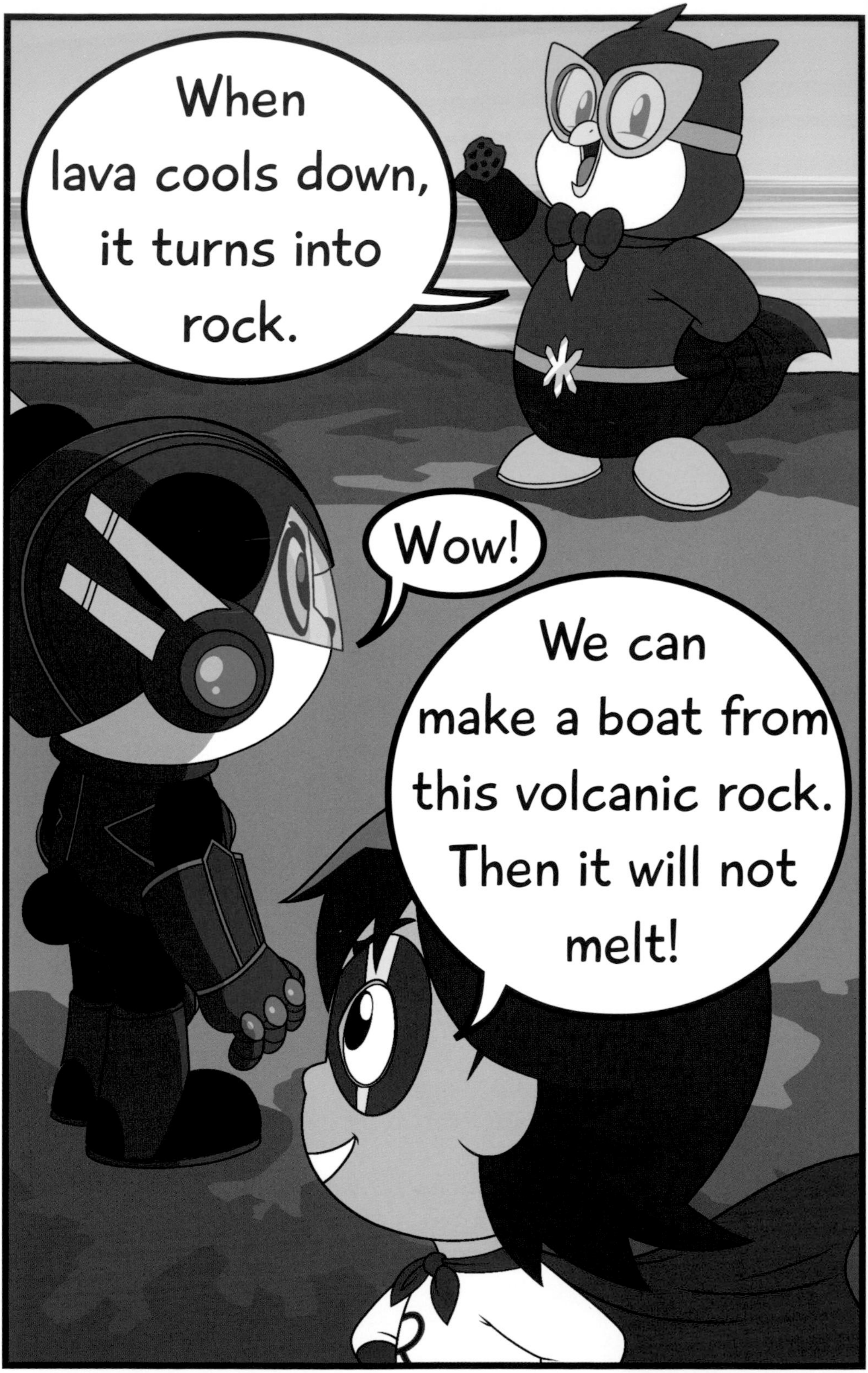
When lava cools down, it turns into rock.
Wow!
We can make a boat from this volcanic rock. Then it will not melt!

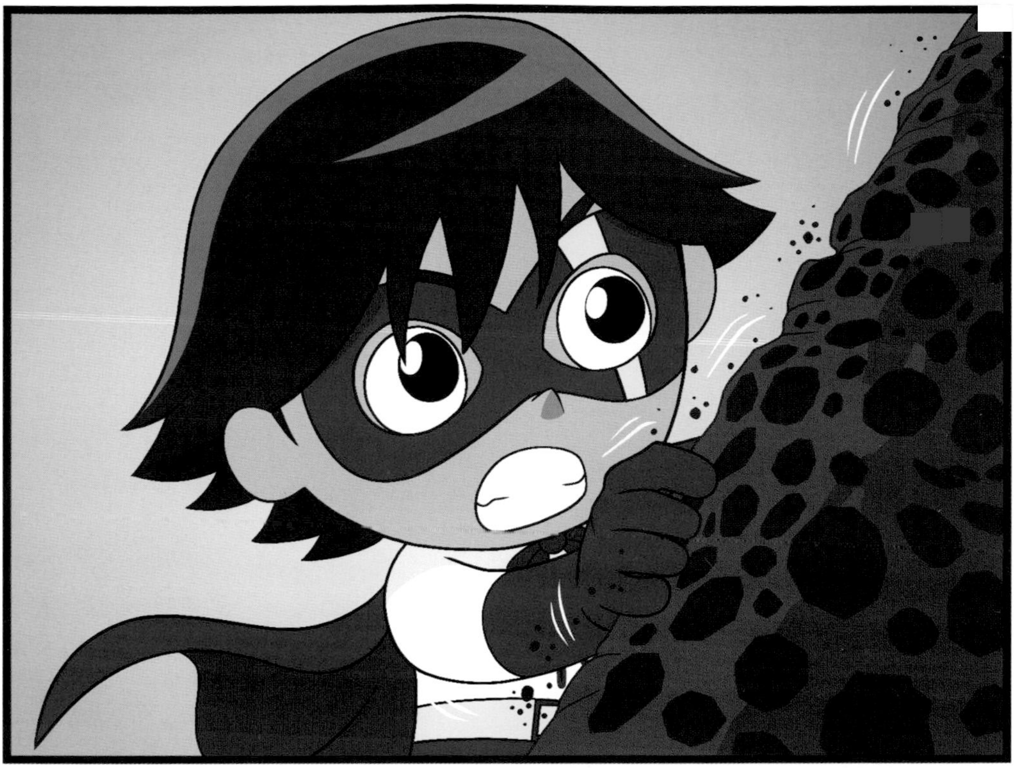

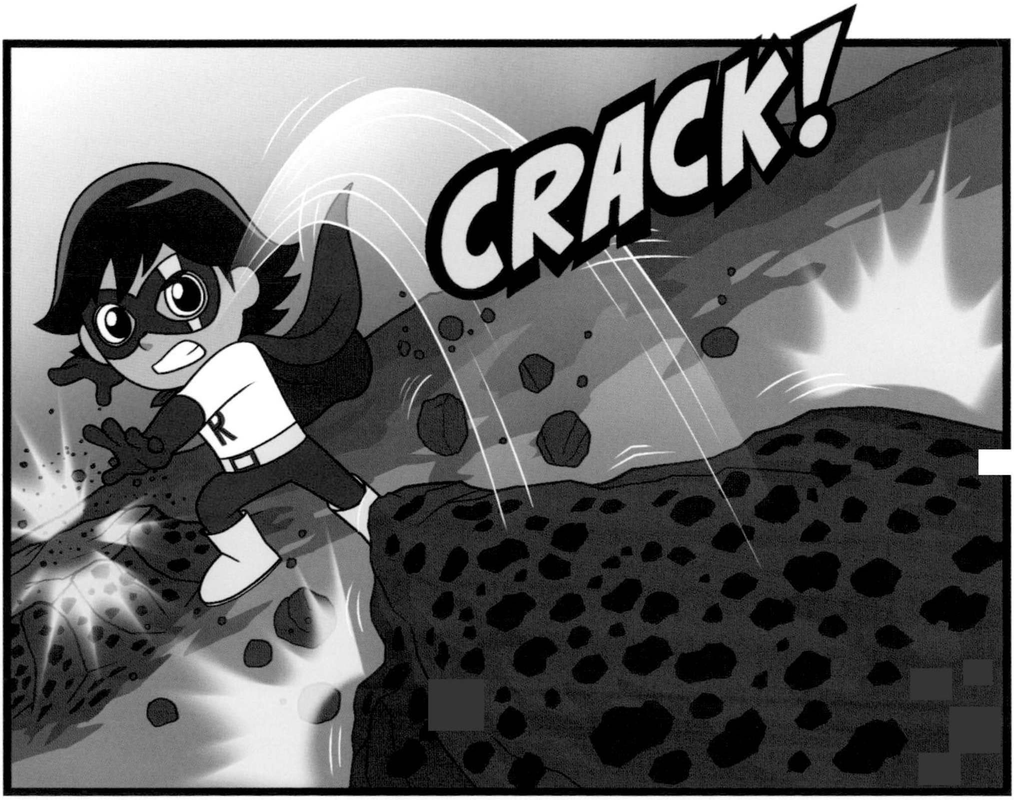
CRACK!

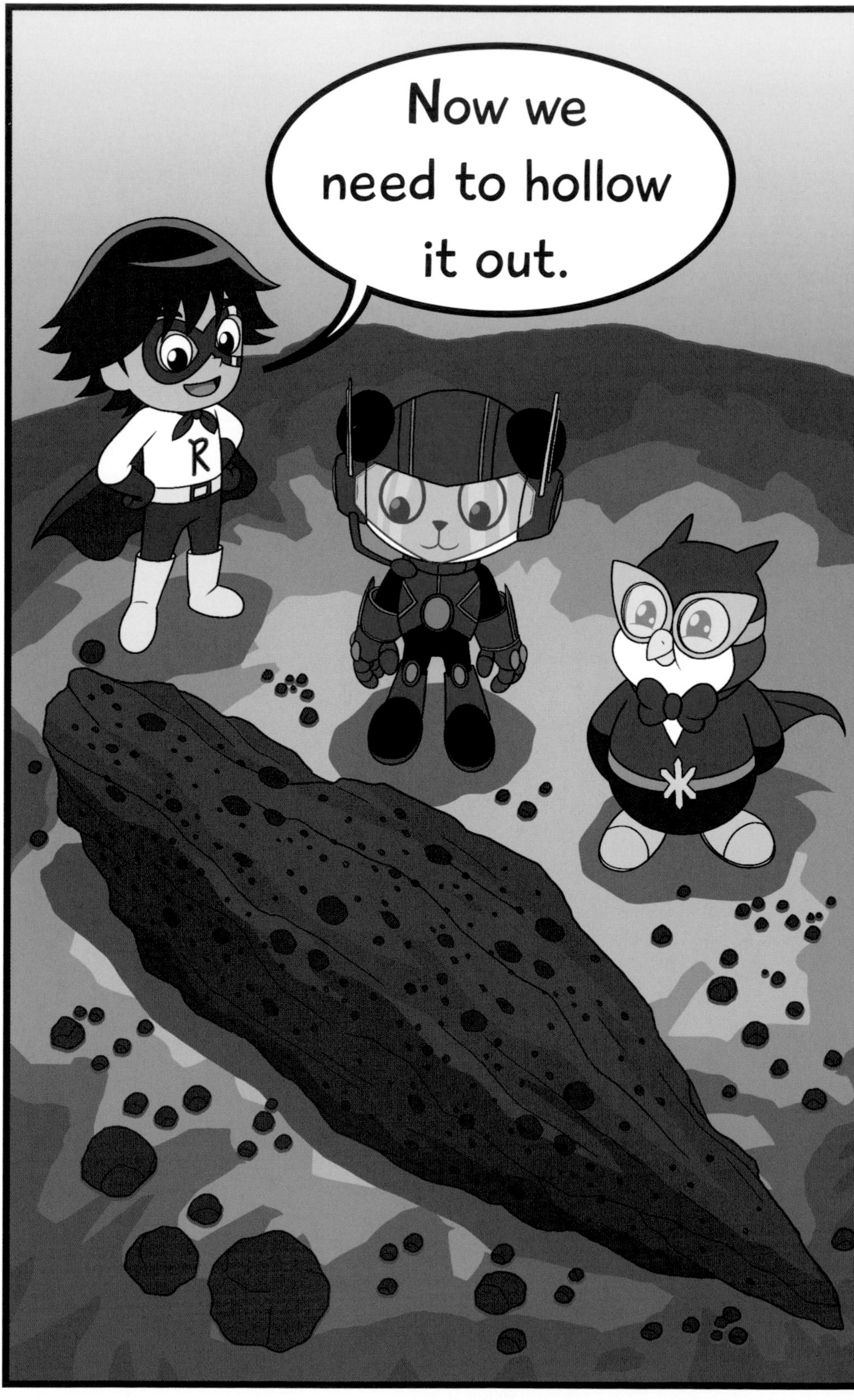
Now we need to hollow it out.

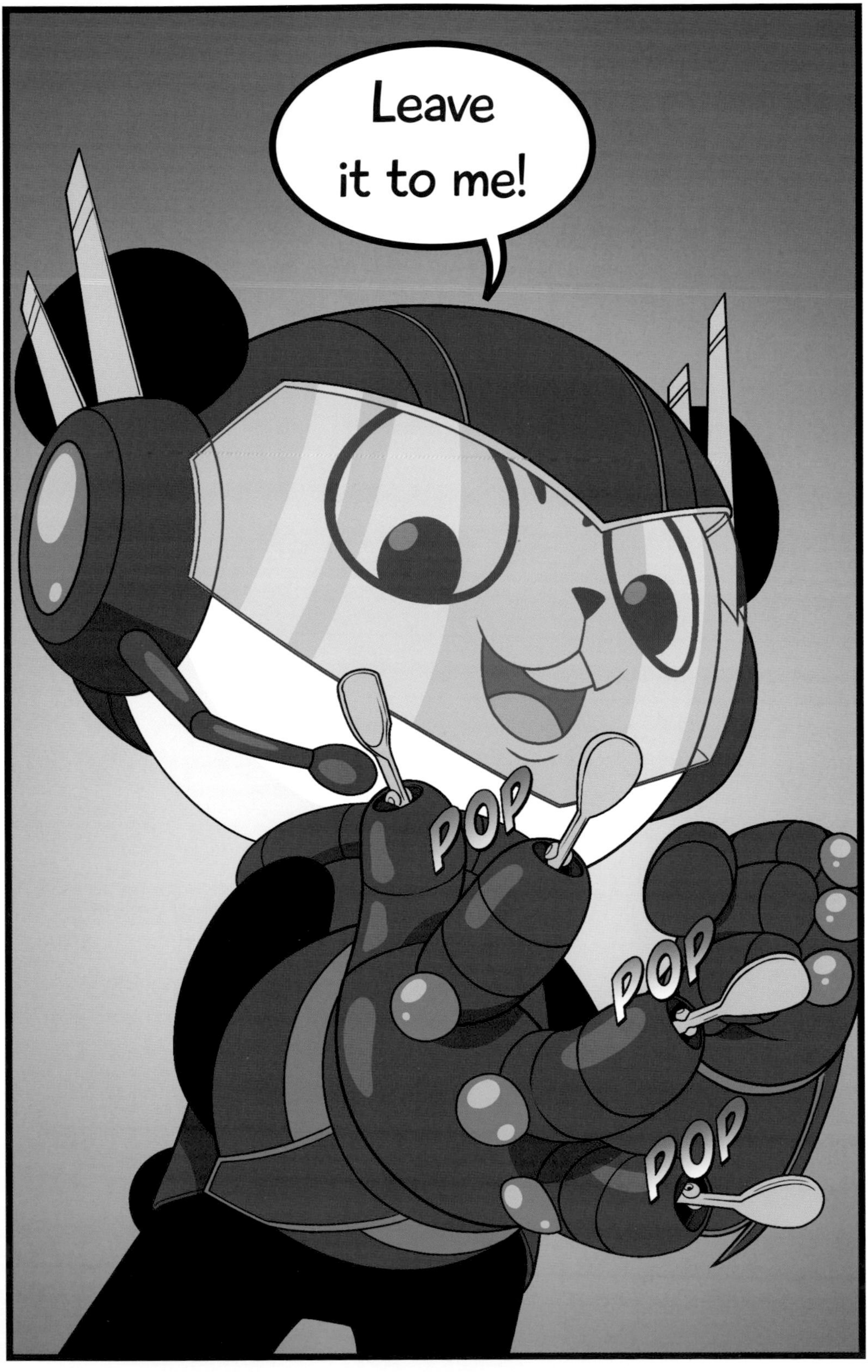
Leave it to me!
POP
POP
POP

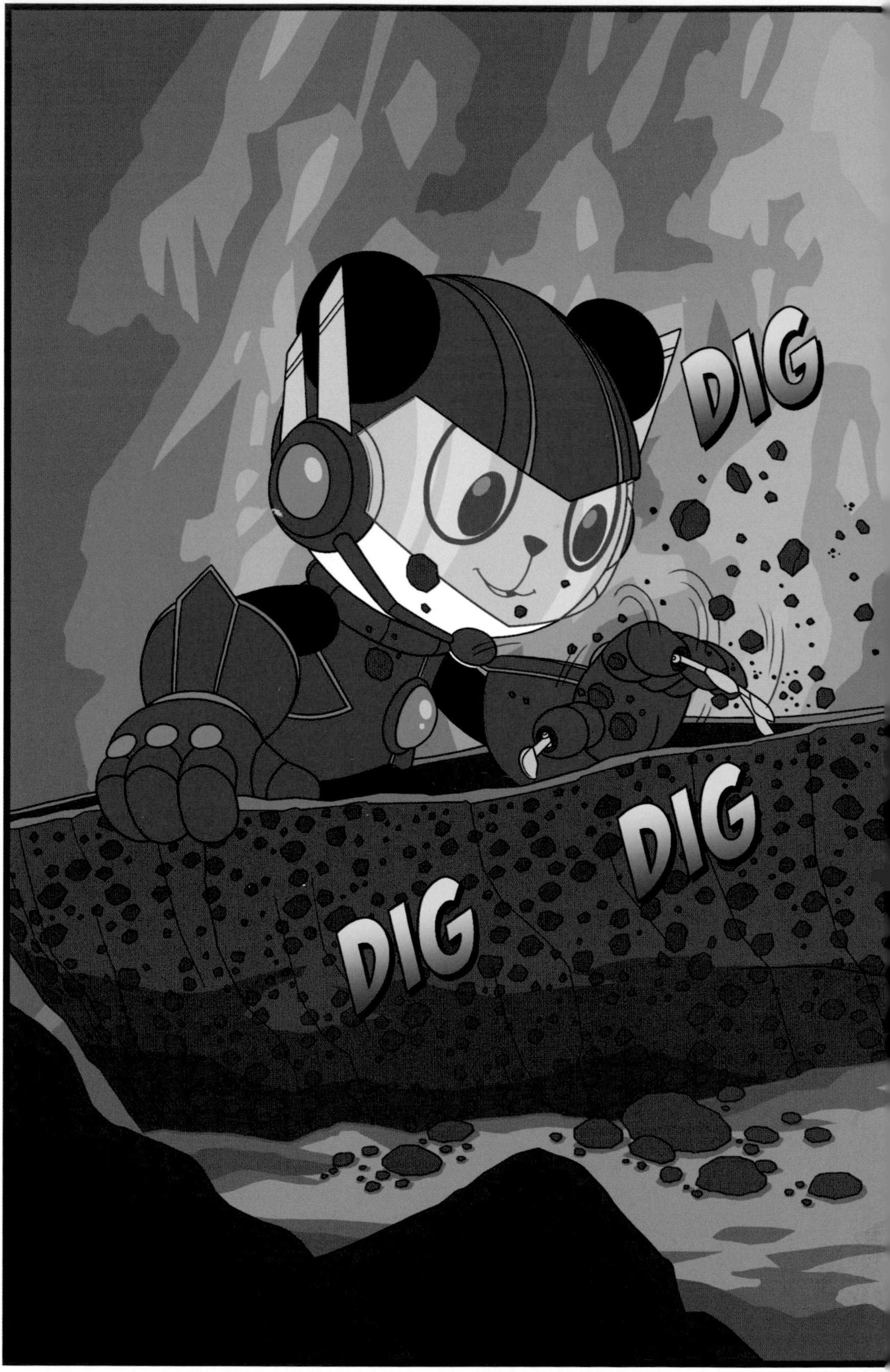
DIG
DIG
DIG

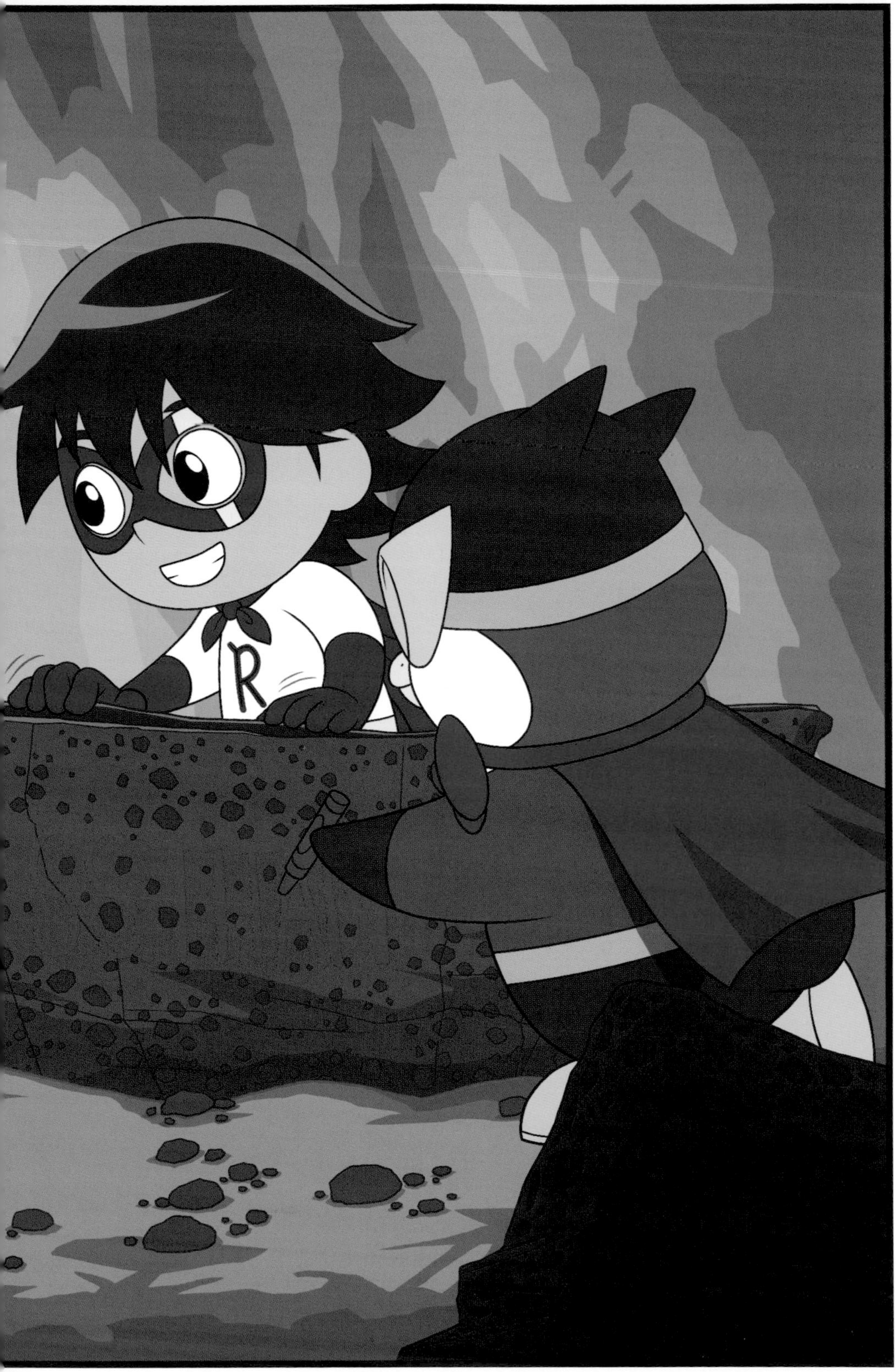

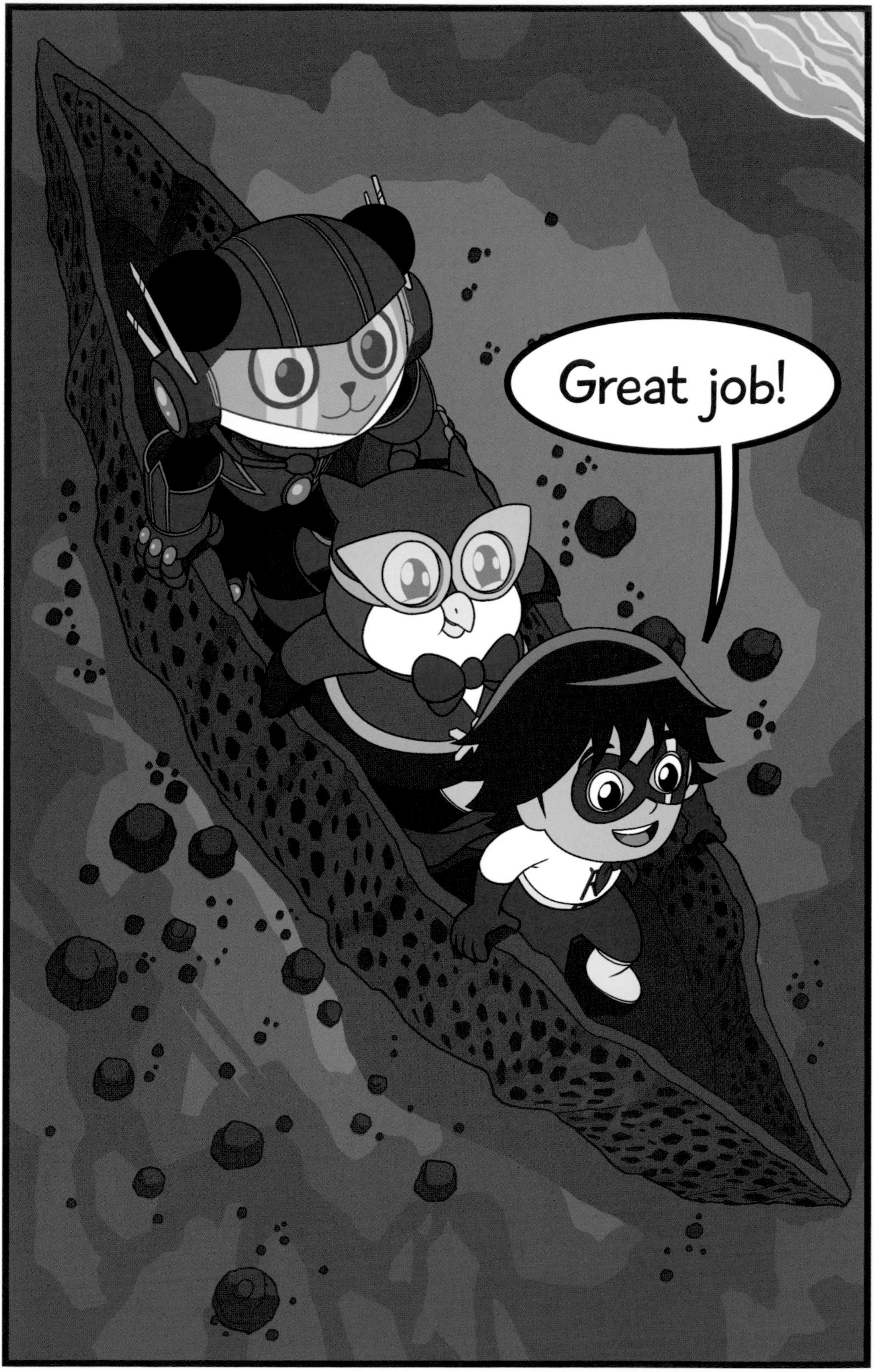
Great job!

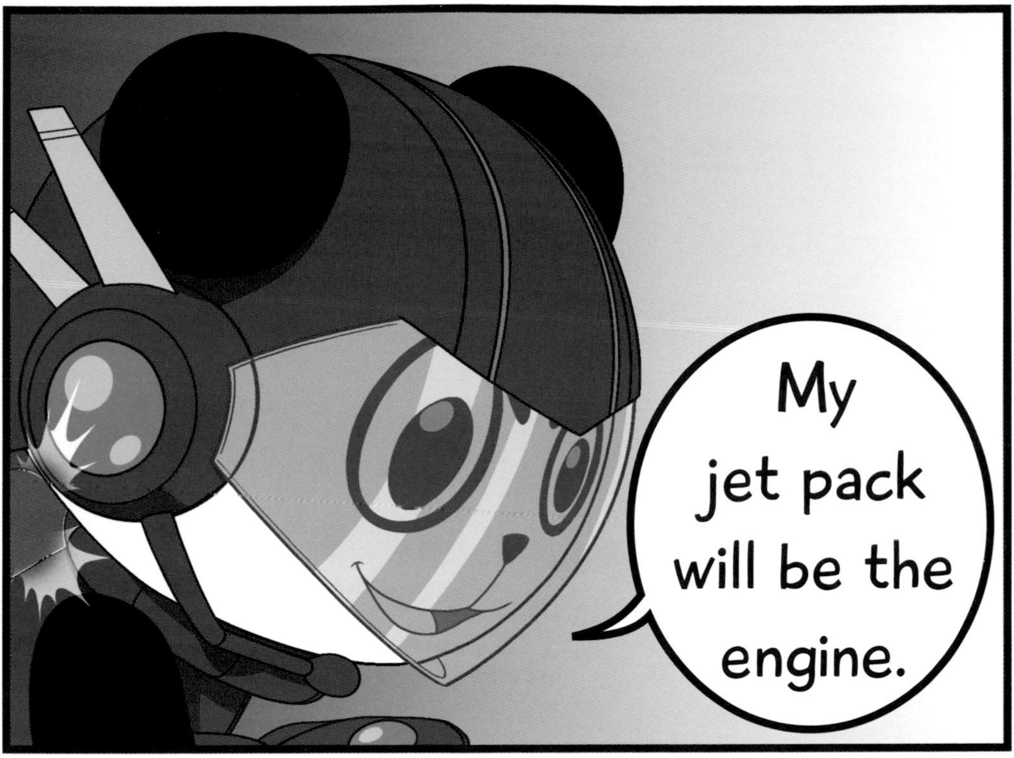
My jet pack will be the engine.

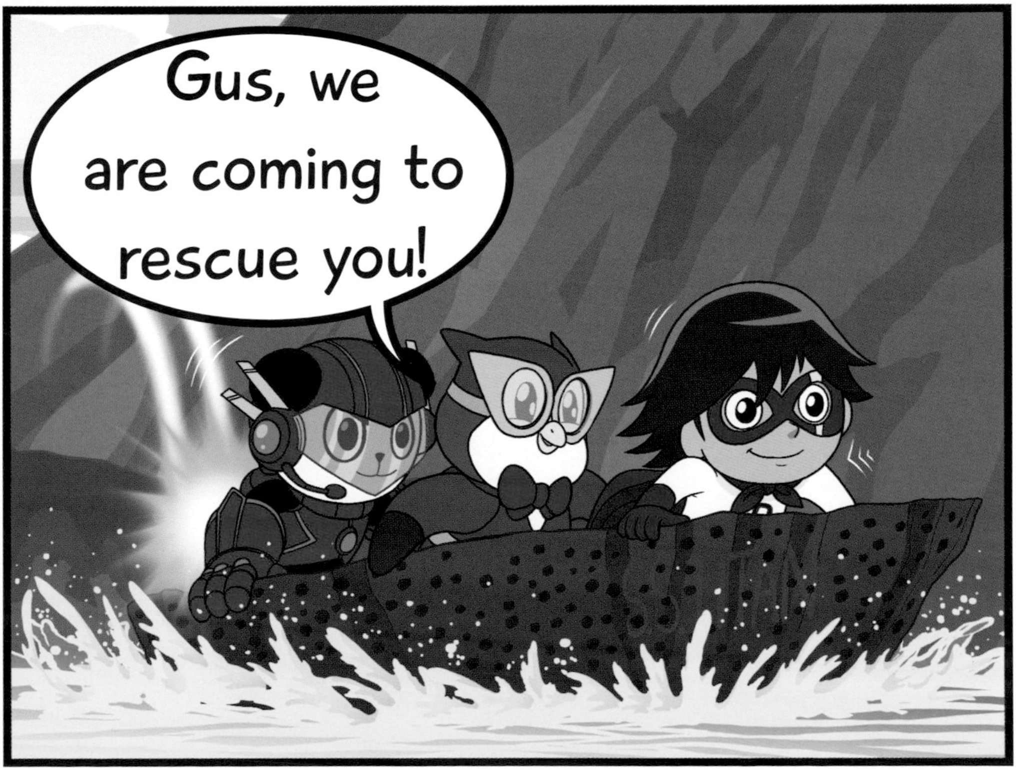
Gus, we are coming to rescue you!

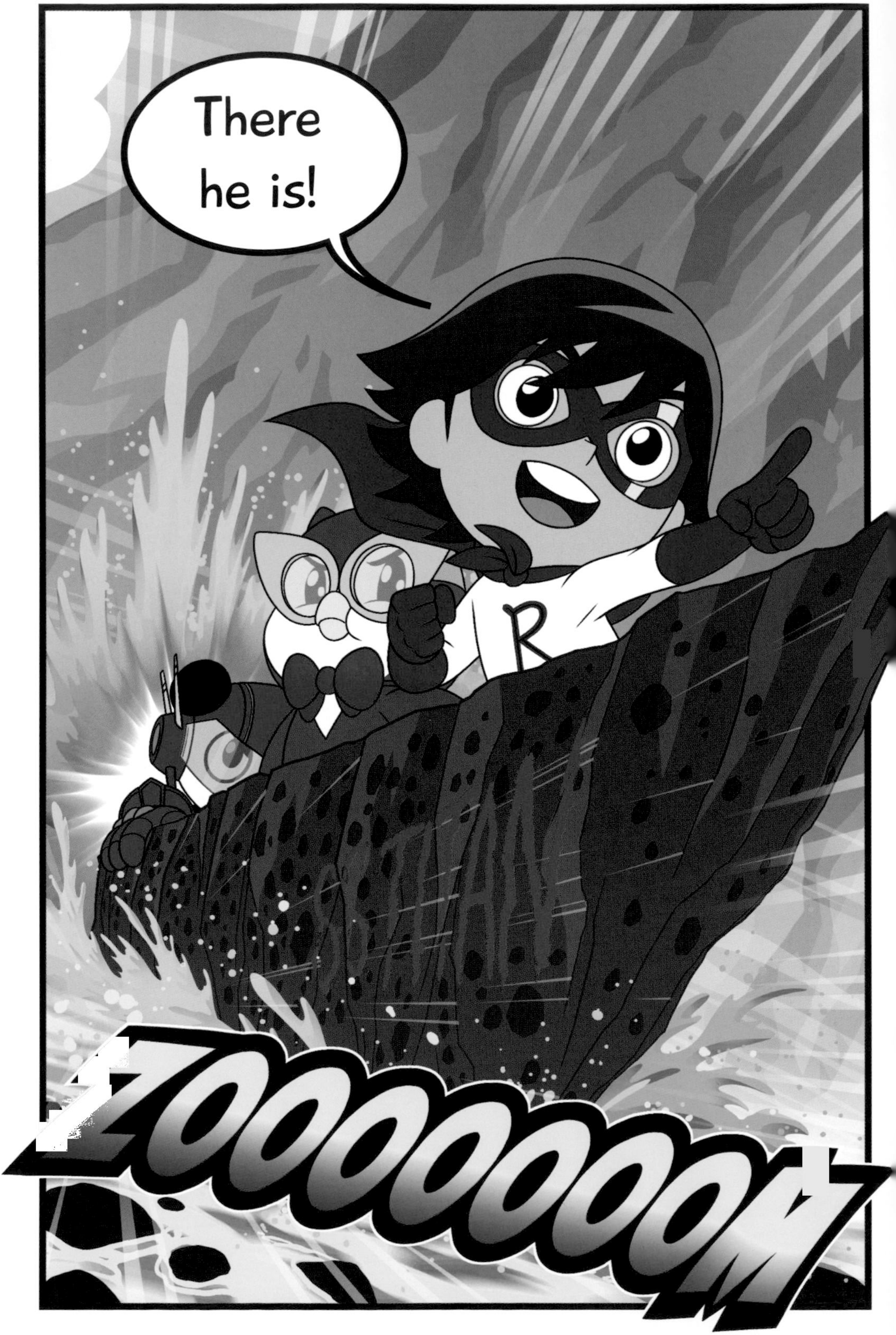
There he is!
ZOOOOOOOM

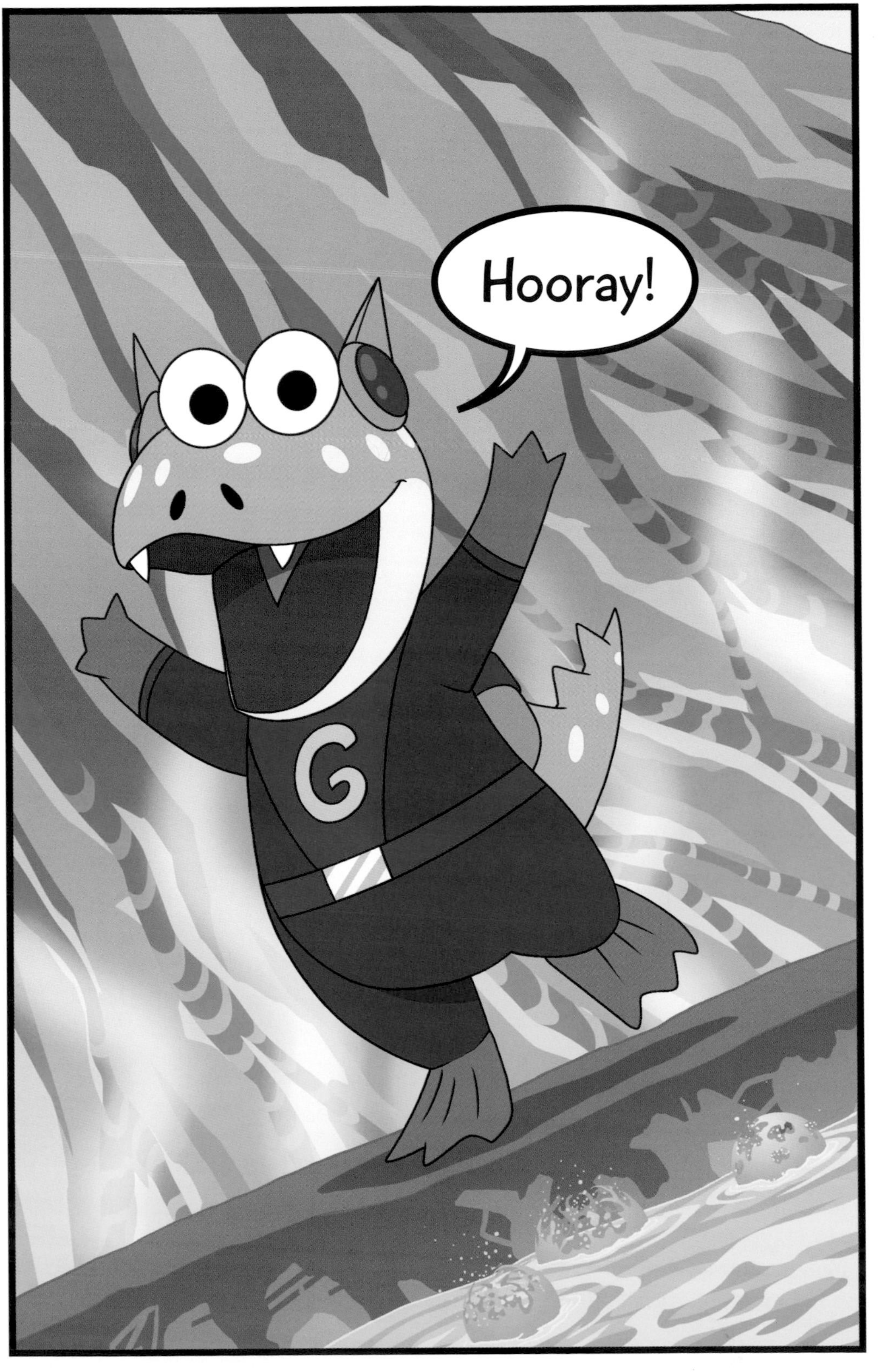
Hooray!

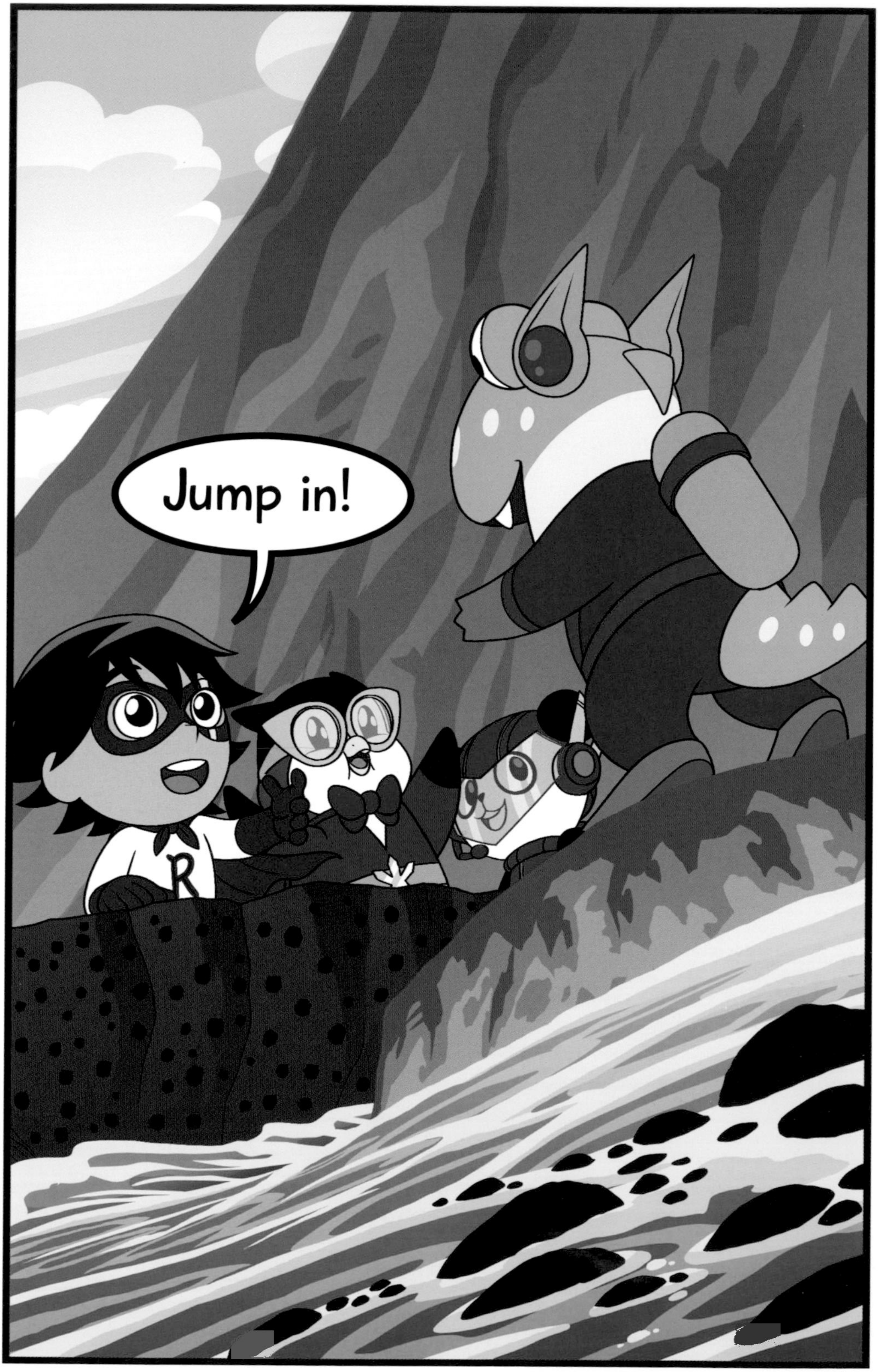
Jump in!

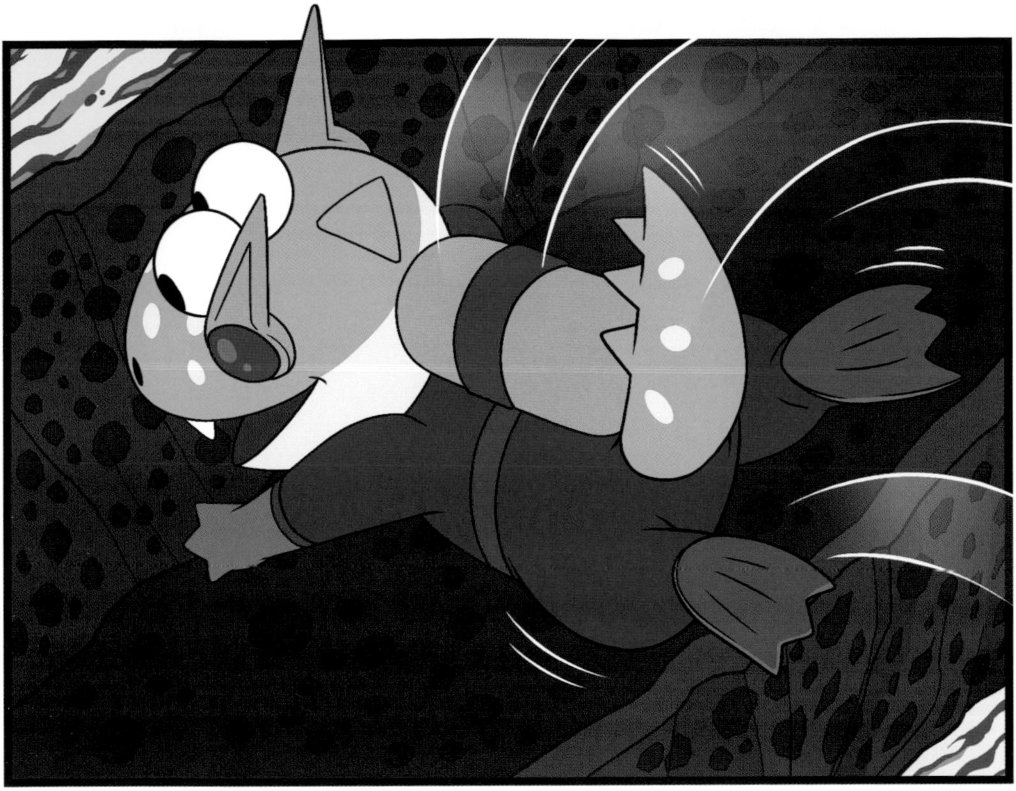

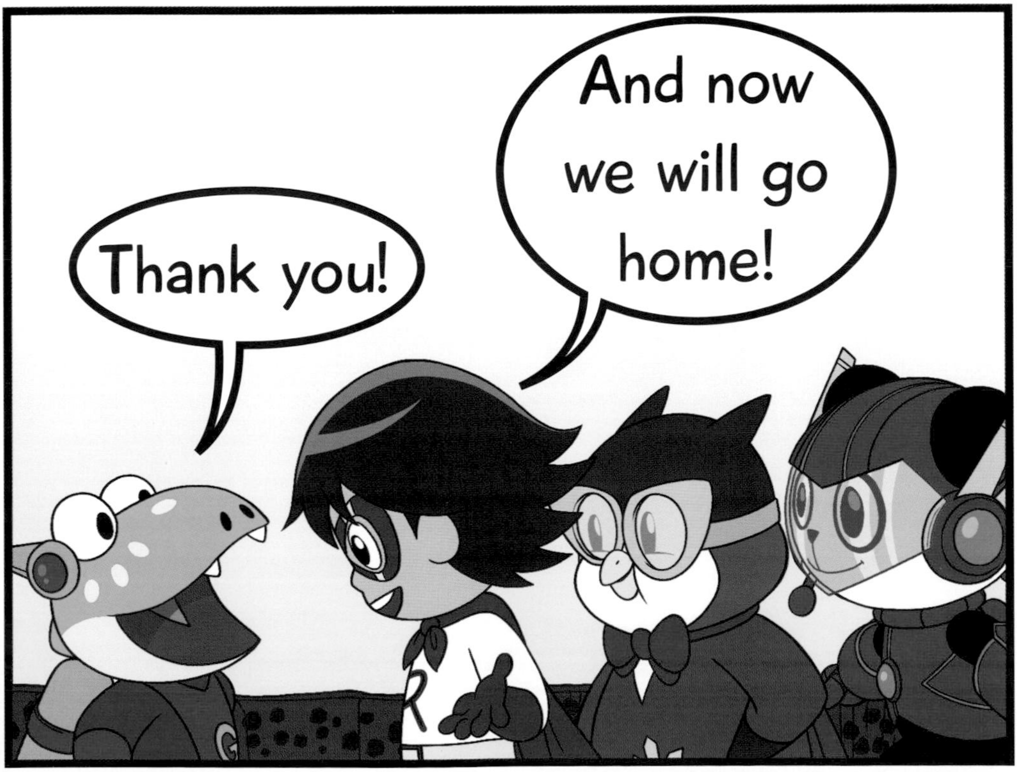
Thank you!
And now we will go home!

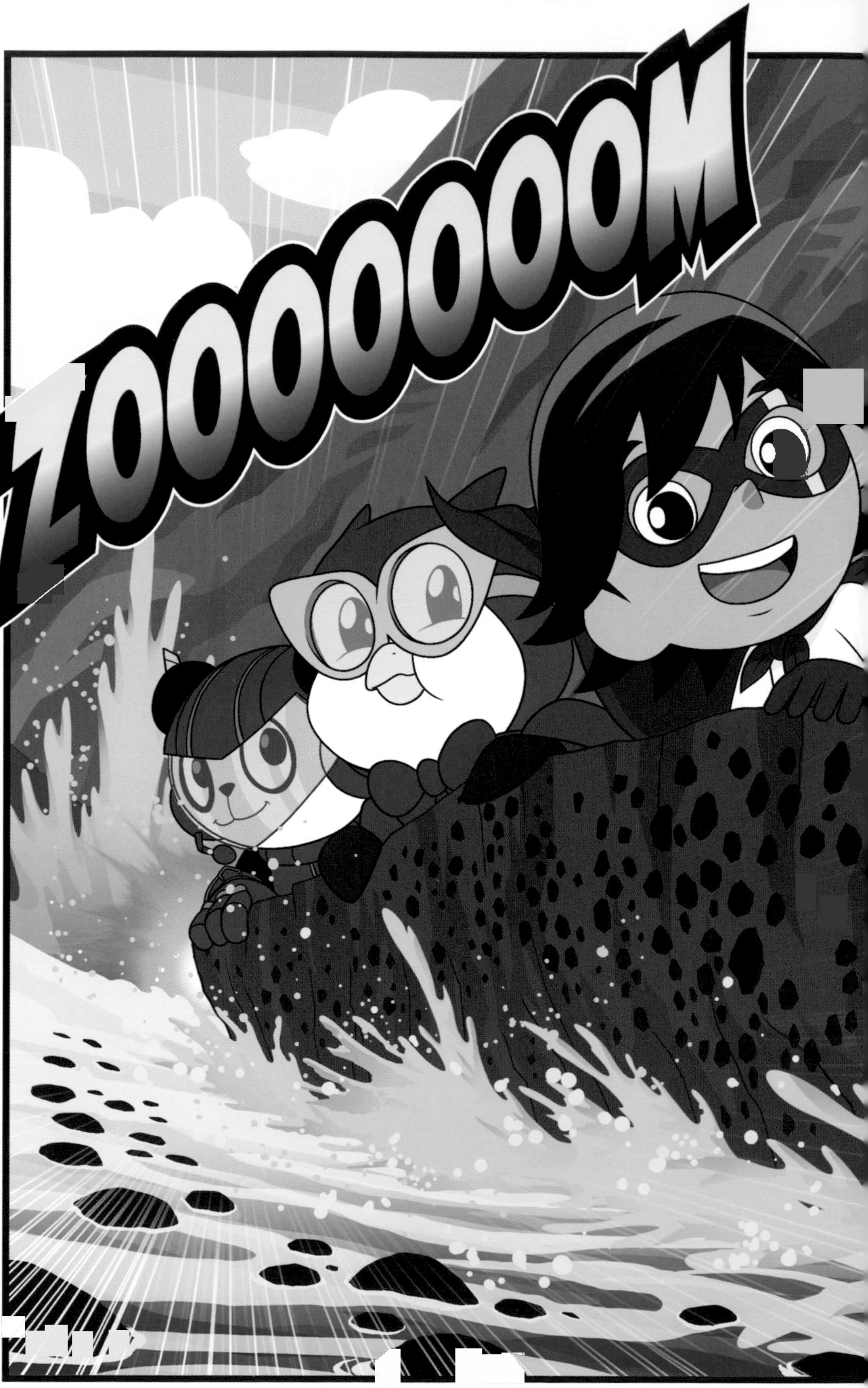
ZOOOOOOOOM

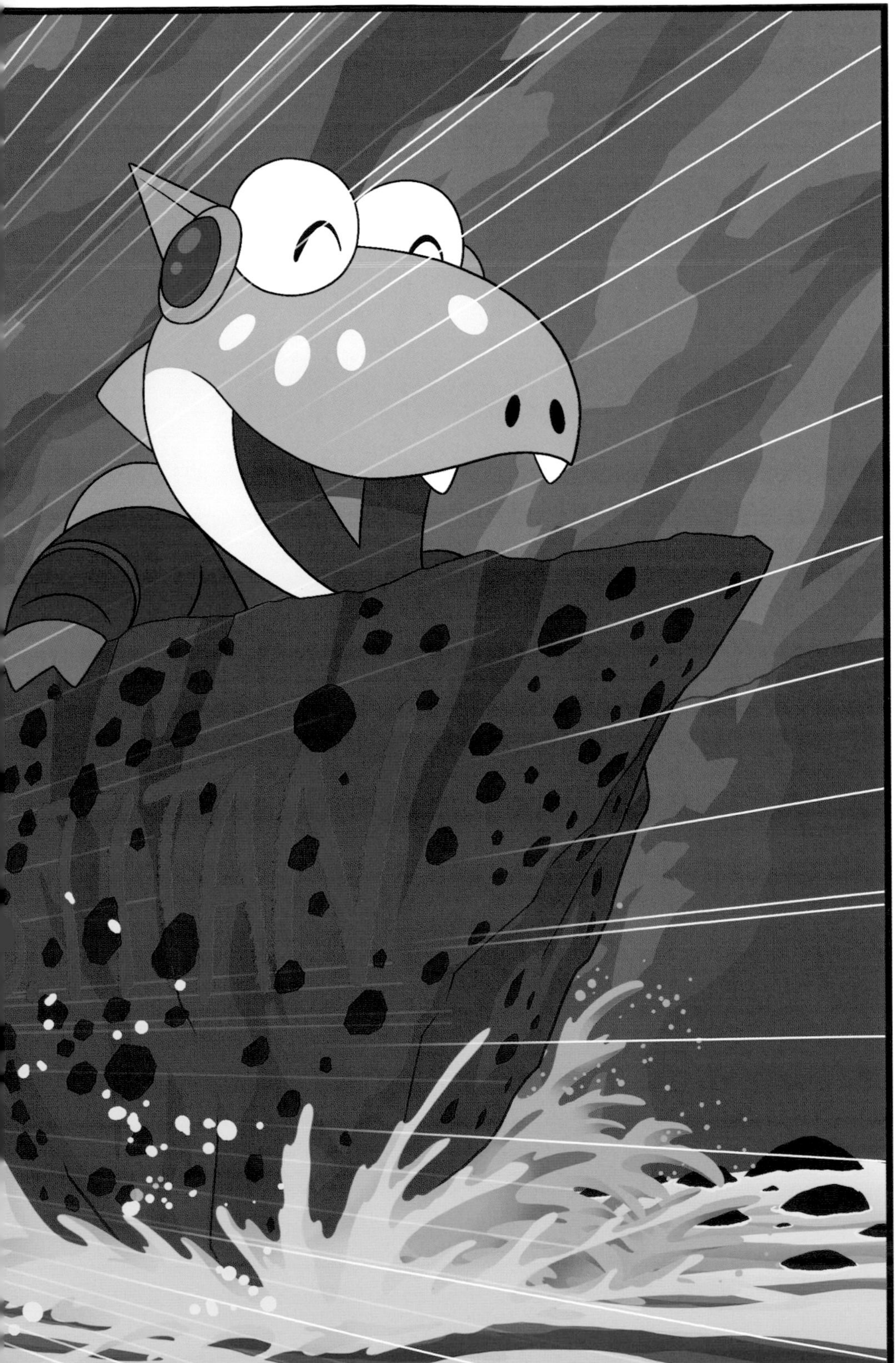

The next day...

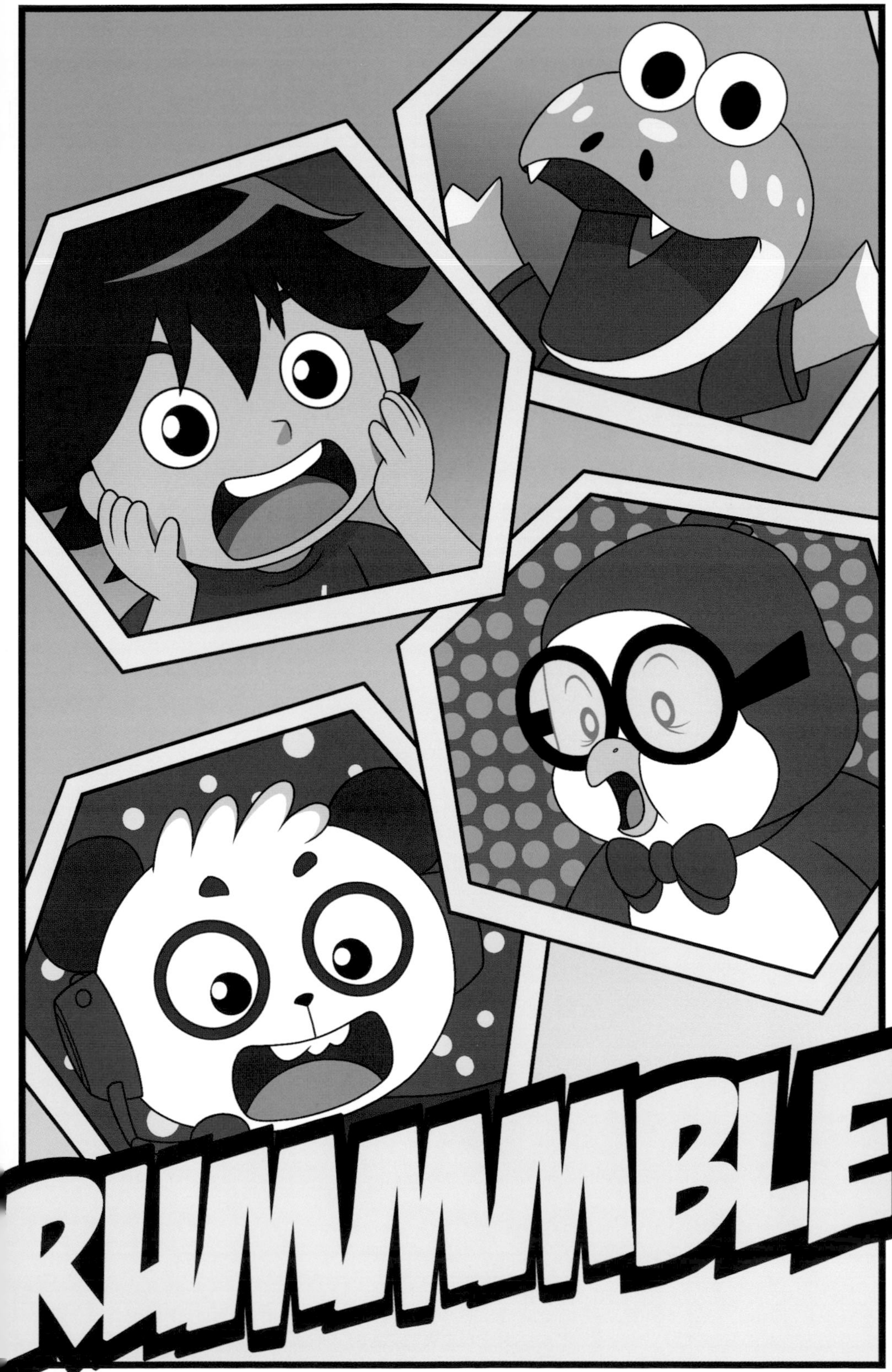
RUMMMBLE

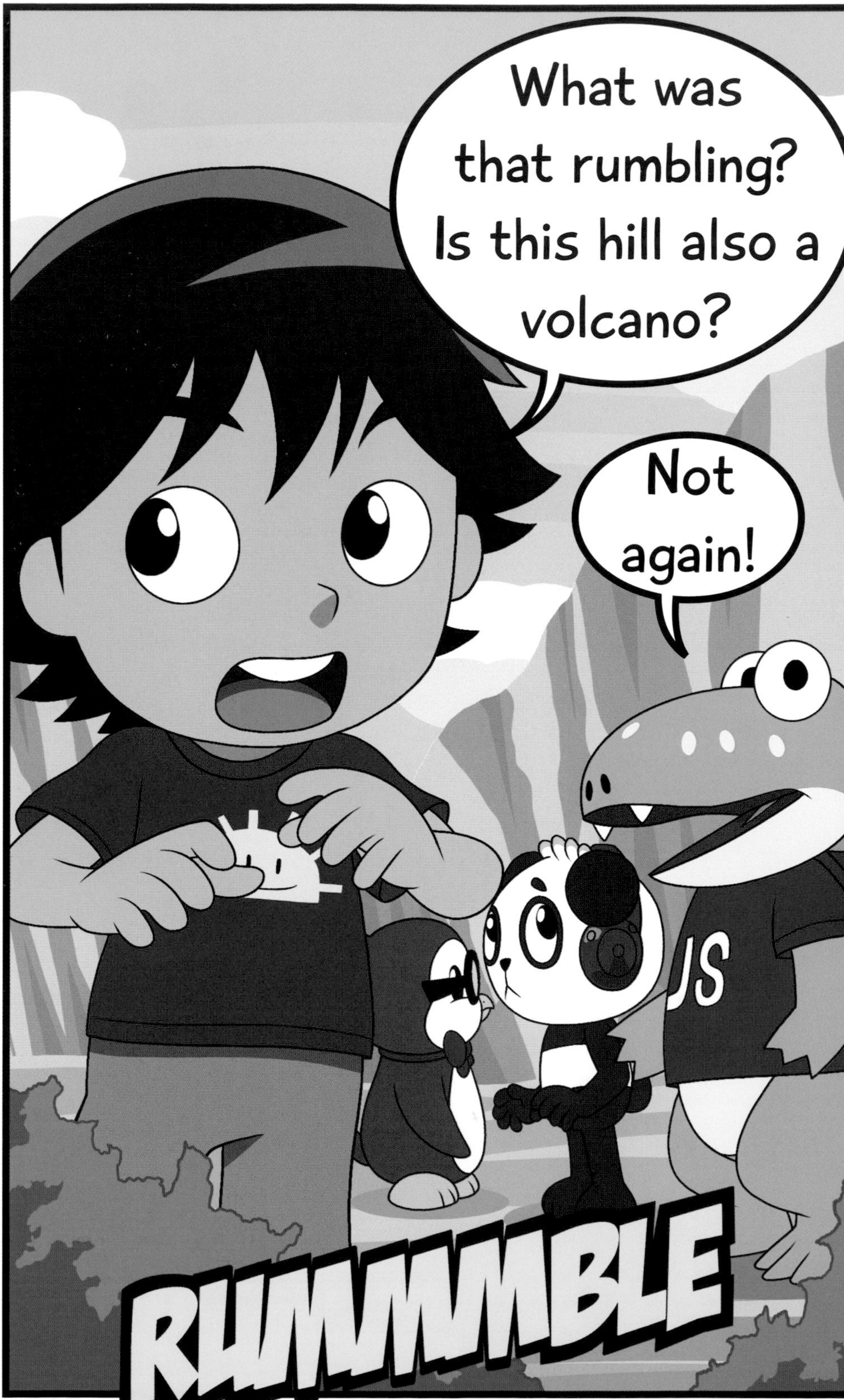
What was that rumbling? Is this hill also a volcano?
Not again!
RUMMMBLE

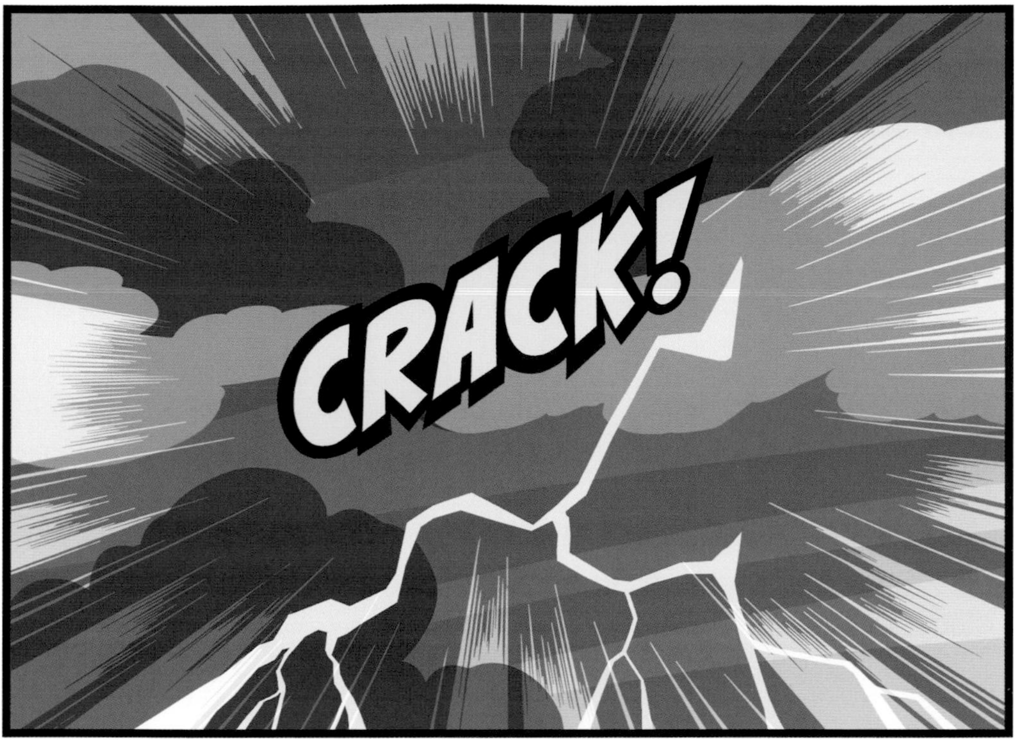
CRACK!

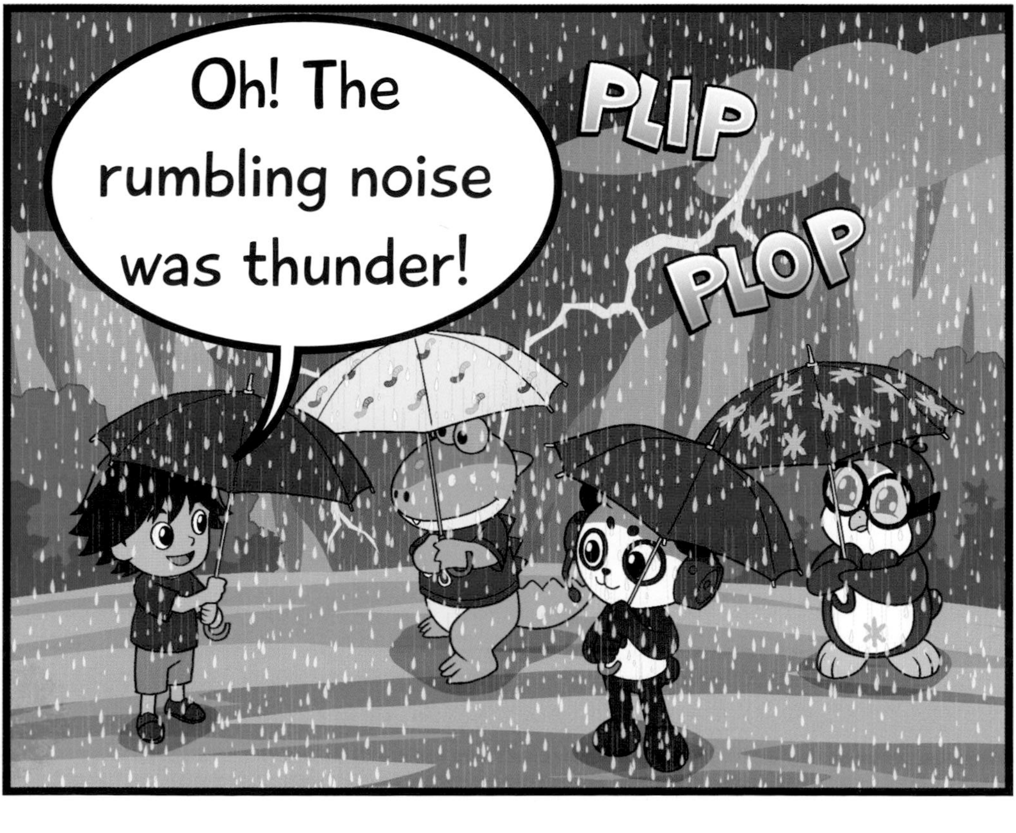
Oh! The rumbling noise was thunder!
PLIP
PLOP

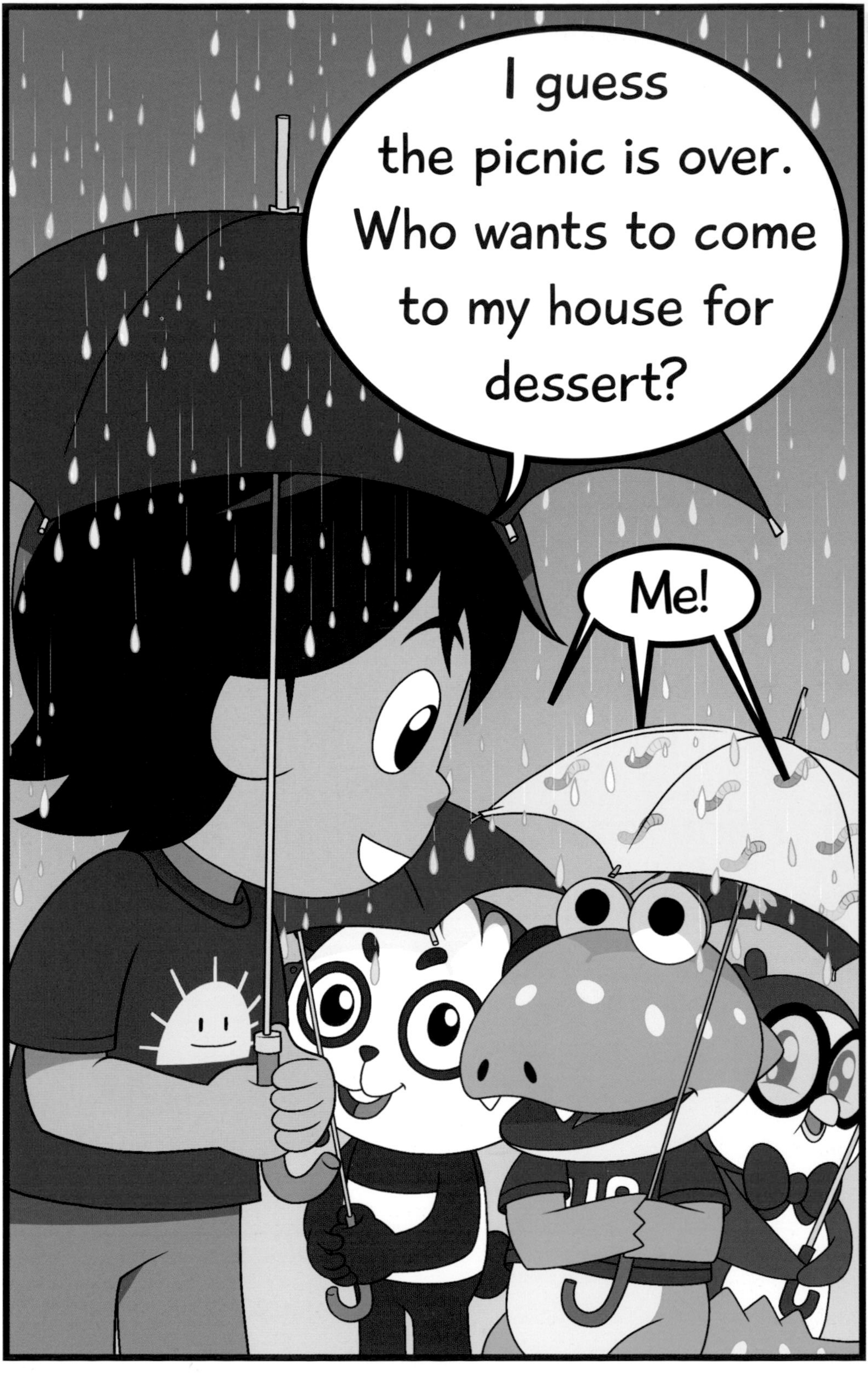
I guess the picnic is over. Who wants to come to my house for dessert?
Me!